Home in Time
for Dinner

Home in Time for Dinner

Kathryn Ellis

Red Deer Press

Published by Red Deer Press, A Fitzhenry & Whiteside Company
195 Allstate Parkway, Markham, ON, L3R 4T8
www.reddeerpress.com

Published in the United States by Red Deer Press, A Fitzhenry & Whiteside Company
311 Washington Street, Brighton, Massachusetts, 02135

Edited for the Press by Peter Carver
Text design by Daniel Choi
Cover design by Francesco Paonessa
Music acknowledgements: "Walk On" written by Steve Dean and Lonnie Williams, performed by Reba McIntyre © 1989 MCA Records; "Okie from Muskogee" written by Merle Haggard and Eddie Burris, performed by Merle Haggard and the Strangers © 1969 Capitol Records; "Walk on Faith" written by Mike Reid and Allen Shamblen, performed by Mike Reid © 1990 Columbia Records.

Printed and bound in Canada by Webcom

5 4 3 2 1

We acknowledge with thanks the Canada Council for the Arts, and the Ontario Arts Council for their support of our publishing program. We acknowledge the financial support of the Government of Canada through the Canada Book Fund (CBF) for our publishing activities.

 Canada Council **Conseil des Arts**
for the Arts **du Canada**

 ONTARIO ARTS COUNCIL
CONSEIL DES ARTS DE L'ONTARIO

Library and Archives Canada Cataloguing in Publication
Ellis, Kathryn, 1955–
Home in time for dinner / Kathryn Ellis.
ISBN 978-0-88995-477-9
I. Title.
PS8559.L558H64 2012   jC813'.54   C2012-900806-0

Publisher Cataloging-in-Publication Data (U.S)
Ellis, Kathryn.
Home in time for dinner / Kathryn Ellis.
[   ] p. : cm.
Summary: A teenager discovers that his single parent dad kidnapped him when he was a toddler and takes a harrowing journey across international borders to find the mother he thought was dead.
ISBN: 978-0-88995-477-9 (pbk.)
1. Teenagers — Family relationships — Juvenile fiction. 2. Adventure stories — Juvenile fiction. I. Title.
[Fic] dc23   PZ7.E5547Ho 2012

Preserving our environment

Red Deer Press chose to print the pages of this book on recycled paper and saved these resources[1]:

	energy	water	greenhouse gases	solid waste
30 trees were saved for our forests	12 million BTUs	52,755 L	1,402 kg	401 kg

Printed by **Webcom Inc.** on Legacy Hi-Bulk Natural 100% post-consumer waste.

FSC
www.fsc.org
MIX
Paper from responsible sources
FSC® C004071

[1]Estimates were made using the Environmental Defense Paper Calculator.

To Yan, of course

MAY 1992

I took the back porch steps in two strides, quickly unlocked the door, and threw my books onto the bed as I passed my bedroom. I was in the kitchen even before the screen door had slammed behind me. If my dad were home, he would have yelled at me about one or all of the above by now, so I knew I'd just managed to beat him.

It was already 5:15, and my dad was usually home by twenty after, depending on traffic, and he expected to see the table set and dinner begun.

It had started out to be a pretty ordinary day at school, and then Brian and I were jogging across the field for baseball tryouts practice. It was one of those hot and sticky days. The sun would bore a hole through you.

After stretches and drills, Coach split us up for a quick five-inning practice game. "Gotta hone those game-situation instincts," he told us.

My team was winning, though I had made no contribution to that. I was playing third base that day and, so far, there hadn't really been any plays there. I had caught a routine fly for the third out in the second, stopped an easy grounder in the fourth, and my two at-bats produced two straightforward outs for the other team. Now I was up to bat for the third time, with two out, no one on base. I rosined up my sweaty hands and swung the bat a few times before stepping up to the plate. As the ball flew toward me, I tried to remember everything Coach had told me about my stance. Just how to stand. Just how to watch the ball. Just how to swing. Concentrate ... and CR-ACK! I had hit the ball square, and hard, and it was sailing high and far. It bounced somewhere behind the shortstop, and I could see the left-fielder desperately running backwards as I went for second base. I could make it a triple. I passed the second baseman and turned toward third, and, just out of the corner of my eye, I saw the fielder bobble the ball. Could I make it? Had I hit a homer? I saw third base ahead, where I could stop and be safe. I slowed slightly, deciding. Safe, or stretch it? I knew I was fast; I thought I could do it, I probably could outrun them, I could stretch it, an in-the-park-homer—*that* would show Coach that I should be on the team, and I poured on the juice and went on through third. And then I saw the catcher positioning himself for a catch. If the catcher was right in his stance, the throw was dead-on. And I hesitated. Instead of pressing for home, maybe having the chance to knock the catcher off balance, blow the play, I hesitated. The next thing I knew, I was caught in a run-down between third and home, I was tagged, I was out, in the most humiliating way.

I wished I were invisible. If I was sweating before, I was oozing now. I should have stayed at third. I should have pressed for home. I should have done *something* right. I had turned a respectable triple, which could have become a run with the next batter, into a mortifying third out. And now Coach was calling me aside. I wished I'd never even tried out for baseball.

"... maybe next year," Coach was saying. "You've got the speed, kid. Why not go out for track this year and work on that. But discipline's important, too ..."

Discipline. As if I didn't get enough of that at home. I knew *all* about discipline. I left the field in disgust, showered, and got into my jeans and T-shirt. As I jammed my Rangers cap onto my head, I reflected on the fact that all the cheerleaders were out there practicing, so Paula—the cutest girl in tenth grade—Paula had probably seen it all, the whole humiliating enchilada. I didn't wait for Brian, who was probably right now pounding a grand slam and making the team, but trudged slowly home, kicking pieces of loose gravel off the sidewalk like Punch Rodriguez at batting practice. Missed one. Like a six-year-old at T-ball.

I glanced at my watch and suddenly realized how late I was. I broke into a run and made it in record time, which was almost funny, if I'd had a sense of humor about it yet. That would have been all I needed, after a stupid day like this, to have to deal with being late home, too.

In the kitchen, I consulted the slip of paper on the fridge door. Tuesday: *pork chops, potatoes, green beans.* Always have to have something green with dinner, according to my dad. Well, it didn't take long to fry up a couple of pork chops and boil some green beans, but potatoes were going to be a problem. I'd have to substitute Minute Rice. My dad created this system—it was efficient and predictable, he always said. Every Friday, the two of us would decide what we'd like for dinner for the week, then Dad would do a big trip to the supermarket and get everything we'd need, and make up little slips of paper so I would know what to get ready each day. On weekends, Dad did the cooking, so it was fair. With just the two of us in the house—"the odd couple," Dad called us—it worked out easiest that way. It was probably fair.

I had the pots of water on the stove and the table set just as he came in the front door.

"Hey, Chris."

"Hey, Dad." I knew I was going to have to tell him about being cut from baseball, so I was kind of steeling myself for that, but then I saw his face go stern even before I said anything. My insides quivered.

"Minute Rice?" he asked.

Oh, no. "I got home a little late." I decided to save the baseball news for later. "And I figured you'd rather ..." But

I gave up trying the excuse. "Sorry, Dad, it won't happen again."

I turned back to the stove to check the boiling pots, but really to hide the shame I knew showed on my face. I wasn't ashamed at having made Minute Rice, and I was getting over the baseball thing, but I *was* ashamed of not being able to stand up to my father. Why did I back down? I kicked myself inside. It wasn't such a terrible thing to do, to cook Minute Rice instead of potatoes. So why couldn't I say so? Why was my father so unreasonable? Why couldn't I just stand up to him for once?

"You're forgiven, son." I heard the fridge door open behind me as my father took out his customary pre-dinner soda. And why did I let myself feel grateful and relieved to be forgiven when I felt so angry?

We didn't talk about anything much at dinner, except for him to tell me I needed a haircut. My dad had some love affair with barbers, his dark, straight hair always trimmed, always in place. I didn't get it. I didn't tell him about being cut from the team—the moment just didn't seem right. After all, "Ramsay men succeed," was one of my dad's favorite sayings.

He went out after dinner, to the gym or something, and I did the dishes. I went to my room to do my homework, but I wasn't in the mood, so I mostly stared at the map of the world printed on the top of my desk.

It was the only thing in my room that really felt like mine, other than the books, and it had been a fight to get it. I persuaded my dad it was educational. Otherwise, the room was painted off-white, like the rest of the house, semi-gloss (easier to clean, according to him). The windows were covered with blue, green, and white striped curtains from Wal-mart that matched the bedspread. However, my desk—well, it was just a Formica-topped desk—but it had the world on it. I'd always loved staring at it, imagining New York City and its amazing World Trade Center, tracing my finger down the Mississippi and thinking of Huck Finn on his raft, or wondering what the U.S.S.R.—sorry, former U.S.S.R, ex-Evil Empire—or Kuwait—a place I'd never even heard of till last year—would be like.

After a while, though, daydreaming just seemed to be an exercise in frustration, and I got up and checked myself in the mirror. The usual inventory: freckles, blue eyes, sandy hair. I must have inherited them from my mother, who died when I was only three, but I barely remembered her. All I knew was her name was Yvonne, maiden name Coleman, like the camp stoves and lanterns. I'd never even seen a picture of her. Pictures clutter up the place, according to my dad. Maybe he was right about that, but I decided he was wrong—I didn't need a haircut, and *Star Trek: The Next Generation* was coming on soon and I could do my homework later, so I went into the living room and flicked on the TV.

It was a few minutes before the show was going to start, and they were showing one of those "true story" shows that my dad totally hates—*America's Most Wanted* or something like that. I sometimes watch them with guilty pleasure when he's out, with the clicker in my hand in case he should come back unexpectedly. This one was about missing people. They had some kid sitting on Santa's knee, wearing a really gooberish-looking snowsuit, and some ominous-voiced announcer was saying that he had disappeared twelve years before, believed to have been abducted by his father after a custody battle. Then they showed a computer-aged picture of what the kid would look like now.

The face on the television screen was the same face I had just been checking out in my bedroom mirror.

A wave of cold rushed through me, then a ripple of heat. Then I sat numb as I became nothing but a pounding heart. A commercial came on, I suppose, and still I just sat there. If my father had come in doing a hula dance right now, I wouldn't have been able to move.

Get a grip, Chris, I told myself. I took a deep breath. The world began to revolve again, clocks started ticking again, traffic sounds from the street trickled in. Of course it wasn't *me*. How could it possibly be? But what an amazing resemblance—I had a double somewhere in the world. Then again, it was only a computer rendition; it couldn't be perfectly exact. But, boy, what a weird thing. And didn't they say it was in Canada, which, as it happens, was where I was born? Maybe I had some distant cousin or something that I didn't know about.

I really couldn't concentrate on *Star Trek: TNG*, and I just sat there in front of the TV. I thought of calling Brian, but when I tried to think of what to say, it just sounded too silly. Maybe I'd casually mention it to him tomorrow at school.

I watched to the end of the episode, though I couldn't have told you what it was about, and then clicked the television off and headed for my room. Even though it was still early, I got ready for bed, and climbed in with an old *Calvin and Hobbes* book, but my mind was still racing and I turned the pages automatically, hardly taking in the jokes I'd read a million times before.

I had a double somewhere. It was the most amazing sensation, having grown up so alone. Maybe some cousin on my mother's side—my dad had no family, an only child himself, with parents long since gone. Or probably we weren't related at all, but just the thought of someone being so like me filled me with—it was a thrill, a tremor, a shivery sensation. It would be so interesting to find this guy, find out what he was like. But then I remembered—no one could find him, not even his own mother. I realized I hadn't even heard what the guy's name was, or anything.

That got me thinking along another line. What would it be like to be kidnapped by your own father? It was one thing for me—no one could help it that my mother had died—but what would it be like for that guy on TV, to be *deprived* of his mother? Did he know he was kidnapped? What kind of a father did he have who could do something like that? What kind of selfish, self-centered father would do that? If he knew, why didn't he tell the cops or something? Obviously, he didn't even *know* he was kidnapped. What kind of lies had this guy's father told him? I turned another page in the book and the shivery feeling came over me again, and a trickle of some kind of a thought I didn't want to know about. I turned out the light abruptly and willed myself to go to sleep.

The next morning, when my alarm went off, I woke up feeling strange, like you do when you know, even before you're awake, that that day there's a big exam, or it's Christmas, or baseball tryouts or something, a sense of anticipation. And then I remembered. All day long at school I kept thinking about it and I kept waiting for someone else who'd seen the show to come up to me and ask me about it. I wondered what I'd say if they did, because I still had this weird, nameless feeling I couldn't put my finger on. I didn't want to talk about it, and it made me jumpy all through classes.

My dad went out again that night—in fact, dinner was on the run (canned ravioli, nothing green, but tomatoes counted), so I still hadn't told him about being cut from the team. I wasn't sure whether he would be sympathetic or mad at me. Probably mad. After dinner, I sat on the back porch steps of the house, one of my favorite spots, and watched the sun begin to go down. It was a perfect spring evening, not too hot, with just a bit of a breeze.

Like the house, there wasn't much going on in our backyard. None of those old rusting cars and bedsprings like some people had, no carefully tended vegetable garden, like Brian's mom fought the Texas sun and soil for. There was a peak-roofed tool shed, gray, and a doghouse, made by my dad for a dog we'd had for a little while. My dad and I never talked about that dog afterwards, but I remembered him very well. He was a mutt the color of September grass, and I called him Rover, which I was thinking now wasn't very original of me. He had followed me home one day, when I was around nine, and my dad said we could keep him till we found his owner but, even though we put up posters and advertised on the free community news on the radio, no one had ever claimed him, so he stayed. Rover was an excellent dog. Never did what you told him to, but he had such a great face you couldn't care. Though it always annoyed my dad that he wouldn't come when you called, I almost think that was what I liked best about the stupid dog. And then, one day, he must have followed someone else home, because we didn't see him anymore. I put up posters and advertised on the free community news on the radio, but no one ever responded. So I cried, figured I never should have named him Rover, and my dad wouldn't ever let me get another one.

On top of the doghouse there was a birdhouse that I made in seventh grade, but no birds ever set up house-keeping there. The birdhouse on top of the doghouse made me think of Snoopy and Woodstock from the comics in a wonky sort of way and I half-grinned at the thought. It was like that double, like my double—why couldn't I get that thought out of my mind? Gradually, I realized that the rattling sound I was hearing was someone knocking on the front door, and I jumped up and ran through the house, just as whoever it was started down the front porch steps.

I swung the screen door open and called out, "Hello?" and the girl turned around.

"Hi, I'm selling chocolate bars for ... oh!" It was Paula. The cutest girl in tenth grade. "I didn't know you lived here." She was smiling.

"Well ..." I tried to think of something to say. "I do." Oh, brother. How idiotic.

"Yeah." Paula grinned back and we stood looking at each other for a minute.

"You're selling chocolate bars?"

"Yeah, they're to get money for new cheerleader uniforms." She waved the cardboard carton she was carrying the bars in.

"I guess that's a worthy cause. I'd hate to see you going around without uniforms." I suddenly had a picture in my mind of all the cheerleaders buck naked, and immediately blushed. "I mean ..."

"I know what you mean." She was still smiling.

"Well, come on in while I get some money." I held the screen door open and stepped back to let her go through. She passed just inches from my chest—the cutest girl in tenth grade—and she smelled sweet, fresh, like soap or clover.

"How much are the bars?"

"Two-fifty." Paula wrinkled her nose, which made her

look even cuter, if possible. "I know. Expensive, right? They're the big kind. I hate selling them, really."

Suddenly, I saw my chance to be her hero. "I'll buy whatever you've got left. How many are there?"

"Six. But you can't do that."

"No, it's okay. My dad loves chocolate." This was a flat-out lie. In fact, he was allergic. I would have to hide the chocolate somewhere or my dad would pitch a fit. "Hang on a sec."

Unfortunately, when I went to the money jar in my room, I discovered I didn't have fifteen dollars. Fifteen dollars of chocolate! Was I crazy? Yeah, crazy about Paula. I knew, though, that my dad had a couple of emergency twenties stashed in his dresser somewhere. I could take one and put it back tomorrow—I doubted my dad would notice, as long as I didn't disturb anything.

"Hang on a sec," I called again, crossing the hall to my dad's room. I could hear Paula humming a little bit of "Walk On"—a Reba McEntire tune, I thought, as I opened the bottom drawer of the dresser. I had never looked through my dad's stuff, but I knew it was probably the bottom drawer, because once when he'd got the money to pay the paperboy, I'd heard the squeak that only the bottom drawer gave.

I carefully moved folded sweaters aside and felt to the back of the drawer for an envelope or something that might be a good place for money. I felt a little guilty—this really wasn't like me, to be sneaking around. I touched something and pulled out a small leather folder, like a wallet, only larger. I unsnapped it and flipped it open. There was actually quite a lot of money tucked among other papers and what looked like the back of a photograph. Clutter, according to my dad. My heart began to beat hard. About the only thing it was likely to be—just maybe—was a picture of my mother. My mouth was dry and my fingers shaking as I flipped the photo over. Was I really going to see her for the first time since I was little? But it wasn't a picture of a woman. I had seen this picture once before. It was Santa Claus, and on Santa's lap sat a little kid in a gooberish-looking snowsuit.

I started shaking all over when I realized what that photo meant. I didn't have a double somewhere. *I* was the kid in the snowsuit who had been taken away all those years ago. Which meant—oh, God, it meant tons of things. It meant that my dad was a kidnapper. And a liar. It meant that my parents were divorced. It meant that my mother was not dead. I just kept shaking. It was like that book, *The Face on the Milk Carton*. I was The Face.

I flipped the photo over again. It was stamped *K. Martin, photog., Market Studio, Kingston, Ont.* Ont. could be Ontario. Ontario in Canada where I was from.

A sound of movement from the kitchen reminded me that Paula was still out there, waiting for the money. I pulled a twenty out of the leather folder and slipped the folder back into the back of the drawer. I was really careful with the sweaters, so my dad wouldn't suspect anything. I closed the drawer and dropped the photo down the back of my shirt. I didn't want Paula to see it, but I couldn't risk it getting folded or crushed in a pocket. I willed myself to be calm, took a deep breath. Catching sight of myself in the mirror above the dresser, I saw that my skin looked white and my freckles stood out like they'd been drawn on me with a magic marker. I hoped Paula wouldn't notice.

"Sorry I took so long. I had to find the money."

"Look, you don't have to buy them all ..."

I brushed her words aside. "I told you, my dad loves chocolate." With super-hero strength, I even managed a lopsided grin. I had to get her out of there, so I could breathe again.

"Well?" Paula broke the silence. "Do you want the box to keep them in, or just the chocolate bars?"

I checked out the box. It would be easier to hide the bars separately. "Just the bars, I guess. Easier to hide. Uh ... for Father's Day."

"Chris?" Paula looked down, then up at my face. "Um ... I'm having a party ... not this Saturday but next ... if you'd like to come?"

A party! There was way too much coming at me these last two days. "Sure," I answered, trying to sound like I got invited to parties every day. I felt dizzy. I was thinking about the photo down the back of my shirt. I had to get her out of there before I started sweating on it.

"Bring Brian, too ... if you like."

"Yeah, okay."

"And ... um ... Chris?" She pointed to the chocolate on the kitchen table. "Thanks."

"No problem."

"So ... I'll see you in school?"

"And a week from Saturday."

"Right. At my party."

And Paula turned and was gone out the door. She didn't let the screen door slam but shut it gently, and I listened to her feet go lightly down the wooden steps.

As soon as she was gone, I pulled my shirt out from my jeans, shook the picture out of my shirt, and tucked my shirttail back in. I scooped up the bars and the photo and went into my room. It only took a moment to stash the chocolate bars in my knapsack— I would take them to school and hide them in my locker. I was pretty sure my dad didn't snoop on me, but I didn't dare take the risk.

I sat on the bed and examined the picture. I had never known what I looked like as a little kid, but it was me, all right. *Now what now what now what?* Keep the picture? Put it back. Talk to Brian? Keep your mouth shut. Where was my mother now? My mother. What a thought. I wondered if it was possible to have so many thoughts in your brain that your head would actually explode.

Calm down, Chris. One thing at a time. The picture. I might need it if I were going to find my mother. But then again, if it were missing from my dad's drawer, he would figure out where I had gone. Wait a minute wait a minute, where was all this thinking coming from? Find? Gone? I had to go find her. My mother. Ridiculous. There was some other explanation for all of this. When I got there, there would be—wait, got where?

Where was I going? Kingston, Ont. was not marked on my desk map, but I found it pretty easily in my school atlas.

It was directly northeast, about 1,600 miles away and over an international border. I needed to talk to Brian. I needed a road map, some money, a bus schedule. I needed a plan. What was I thinking? Just ask my dad. But wait ... what? If any of this was true—any of what?—he'd never give me a straight answer. *Wait, wait, wait! Wait.*

"Are you out of your mind?"

This was at least the fourth time Brian had said that to me today. First, when I asked him to pretend he was sick and skip baseball practice. I was off the team, so I didn't have to go anymore, but Brian was still on (not a grand slam, but a solid hit, after I left). Second, when I told him about the TV show. Third, when I told him about the picture. This time he said it three times over, the first two with the emphasis on the word "mind," the third time with a nice dramatic crescendo on the word "out."

I *was* out of my mind all night and the next day at school. I couldn't think about anything else, couldn't get my mind around this strange new circumstance, did no homework, heard nothing at school. I had gone straight to bed again on Wednesday, so as not to have to deal with my dad. Our morning routine didn't usually involve much interaction and I made sure it stayed that way today. I couldn't think straight, at least until I talked to Brian.

"You're going to *run away*?" We were sitting in a vacant field on the edge of town, where tall grass and an old metal barrel hid us from view.

"Yes, let's tell everyone in Texas, why not?" I indicated the general population with a wave of my arm. "And it's not running *away*, it's running *to*."

"Running to what? You don't even know if she's still alive."

"Of course she is," I pointed out. "Or else why would they be running me on *Missing Kids*?"

"You don't even know if she's still *in* that town."

"Brian, she is, she is. She's still looking for me. She'd stay put where I can find her."

"Why don't you just go to the cops?"

"Yeah, you're right, that's what I should do." I sighed, but I didn't mean it.

"Yeah, you see. It's not you, anyway. Like ... that just doesn't happen to people."

But I wasn't listening. I was still back at the cops. "You don't think he's got it covered with the cops? He must have a story ready, just in case—hell, he might even have a bag packed, for all I know. Mexico's just a few hours' drive. Besides, I don't trust the cops. You never know with them. That's what my dad—well, I guess I know why now. But I still don't trust them. Brian, I just have to *go*. I have to *go* there. I have to find her myself. Should I do it? You have to help me."

Brian took off his ball cap and ran his hand through his hair before putting it back on. He sighed and shook his head. "I can't make you see any sense, can I? You. Should. NOT. Run. Away."

He's right, I was thinking. I can't even trust my own

judgment on a baseball diamond, or making dinner, much less on a cross-country trek. I can't do this. I just looked at Brian, realizing he was right.

"I can't understand this. I thought ... I thought ... I knew. But ..."

I shuddered. I wanted to cry. It was like my whole life had turned into a sandcastle in a hurricane. How could I explain this to him? My best friend in the world ... felt like my only friend. We had grown up practically brothers, going to his place after school, weekends camping with his family, his mom teaching us how to make chili or plant a plant. Going to our first concert together (Garth Brooks). If he couldn't understand this, maybe I really was out of my mind.

I looked at him, feeling helpless.

And then Brian sighed again. "All right, then, what do you want me to do?"

Yesyesyes! I took a deep breath. I'd already given it a bit of thought. "I need a plan, and I need a cover, to give me time to get away. I've done some research on bus timetables"— okay, a call from the payphone at school at lunch—"and there's a bus that goes in the mornings. I was figuring on going Saturday morning 'cause if I skipped school, I'd be missed faster ..."

Brian was just looking at me.

"I need a cover. I need a reason to be away this weekend."

Brian gave me a half-grin. "My dad and I are going camping this weekend."

"I could say I'm coming with you."

Brian nodded, then shook his head. "But what if your dad checks with mine?"

"He probably won't. It's pretty normal."

It was true. Brian and his dad went camping a lot of weekends, and sometimes I came along—often enough that my dad was used to it.

"What if I ask my dad if you can come and then, at the last minute, we tell him you can't make it? Then, even if your dad checks—" Brian clicked his tongue.

"That might cover it ... I could be gone two days before my dad would even notice."

Once I actually had decided, I felt a lot calmer. Okay, I still couldn't concentrate on anything *else*, but I could focus on figuring out how to get to the bus station downtown and how much money I'd need and stuff like that.

Brian helped me plan and lent me some money, and, in a couple of days, I was ready to go. We even used me getting cut from baseball. I never had told my dad about it, so, when my dad reported me missing, Brian was supposed to tell them I was upset about being cut from the team and had taken off for New York City. That way, if anyone saw me heading north, it made sense. And it seemed to me that New York would be an impossible place to find someone in. Especially if they weren't there. It would buy me time.

It was a risky plan. A lot could go wrong. But it was the best we could come up with.

I put the picture back so my dad couldn't figure anything out. And then, on Friday, after he had left for work, I slipped back into his room and took the picture after all.

The sun was up and ravens were squawking from the power lines, but otherwise the world was quiet, quiet, as I stood at the bus stop, waiting for the first bus of the day. It was amazing everything could be so peaceful when I felt so jangled up inside. I thought of all my friends and their parents and brothers and sisters, and I could picture them lying under or out of their covers, an arm off the bed, or curled tight, hair tangled over the pillow, or a mouth hanging partway open, snoring, or dreaming, or stirring, just starting to feel the light of the morning. A car door slammed somewhere far away. An early shift, or a late date, or someone going fishing. The local bus rumbled round the corner and huffed to a stop.

"Y'all are up early, son," said the bus driver.

"Catch the worm," I replied, friendly, but I went to the very back of the empty bus to take a seat. The bus wound into the suburban streets that were so familiar (our house was right on the edge of the city, but suburbs came next, on the way to school). More people were around. A few little kids playing outside. A guy washing his car, of all things. The bus stopped for a fat lady in a nurse uniform. A girl in cut-offs sat on her front steps, painting her toenails red. While the lady took her time climbing the bus stairs, I watched the girl, because it was Paula. I put my hand on the window of the bus, catching her image in my hand, since I wouldn't be at her party a week from today. I wouldn't ever see her again. *I can't do it. I can't do it!* Half of me wanted to run off the bus. But I didn't move. Paula looked up, looked right at the bus, as though she felt me watching her. But she didn't see me—I was hidden behind my hand. She looked back down to dip the brush into the nail polish bottle, the bus pulled away and I closed my hand to hold onto my picture of her.

It hadn't been too hard to slip away. Thursday evening, I had told my dad I was going camping with Brian. He asked me where and I told him Lake Texoma, where we usually went, but he didn't ask anything else. Easy!

"Better decide on next week's menus tonight, then," was his only real comment.

It had felt really weird to be choosing food that I knew I wouldn't be eating. Based on what was on sale that week in the grocery store flyers, we made the plan. Tacos for Monday, my favorite. Tuna casserole on Tuesday, meatloaf Wednesday, chicken Thursday, and pizza Friday. Where on earth would I be by the time my father was eating Thursday's chicken?

Friday morning, I watched my dad eat cereal and read

the paper. How could he be so calm? I wondered how he wrapped his mind around taking me, back then, but stopped that thought. This was hard enough. Don't think.

"Enjoy camping," he said, picking up his keys and heading for the door. "See you Sunday."

"Thanks!" Too enthusiastic? The door closed behind him. "Goodbye, Dad," I finished quietly, then swallowed. Well, that was weird.

It had been pretty easy to get my stuff out—after all, I was supposed to be going away for the weekend, and my dad would never notice if I packed a little heavy. It wasn't that much—if it didn't fit in my backpack, I wouldn't be taking it. Nice to have an excuse to take my sleeping bag and some other camping stuff, too—might come in handy sometime along the way. Well, not really, since I would be on the bus, but I just liked that stuff and it made me feel good to have it with me. Sleeping bag, flashlight, spork. It would have looked weird to go camping without it, anyway. Stuffed in my jean jacket and my Rangers ball cap, shaving kit with shampoo, toothbrush and toothpaste, deodorant.

Friday, I checked to make sure there wasn't anything too disgusting left in my locker, and I stuffed the chocolate bars I'd bought from Paula in the backpack. I went to Walgreen's and bought a roadmap of Eastern U.S.A., and the bottom part of Canada was included on it. I had dinner at Jack-in-the-Box (spicy chicken sandwich, curly fries), since the kids from school didn't generally hang out there, and I didn't want to have to answer any awkward questions.

I'd been jumpy all day at school. I couldn't believe I was actually going to do this. The bell finally rang and I met up with Brian at our lockers, which were next to each other.

Brian handed me his house key. "Wow, I can't believe you're going through with this." He shook his head.

I could hardly believe it either, but I was determined not to chicken out. "I'll leave the key in your nightstand."

"Call me when you get there, if you can."

"I will."

"I gotta get going—my dad's probably waiting."

"Yeah. Catch some big bass stripers for me, okay?"

"Chris?"

I looked at him.

"Um, what if ...?"

I shook my head. "Catch ya on the flip side."

"Take care, buddy. Good luck." We punched each other on the shoulder, and then I was on my own.

After it got dark, I snuck into his house. I was too scared to even take off my shoes or turn on any lights. I just lay down and slept, if you could call it that, on Brian's bed. I didn't even dare to set an alarm clock, in case someone heard it, and I was terrified of sleeping too late.

As soon as it started to get light out, I snuck back out of the house, leaving Brian's key in the drawer of his night-stand, like we'd arranged. Nothing was open, so I had a chocolate bar for breakfast while I waited for the bus that would take me to the Greyhound station, which was right in the middle of Dallas.

The suburbs gave way to bigger buildings and even sky-scrapers, and soon I was at the bus station, which smelled of diesel fumes and fried food. I was about an hour early for the bus to Tulsa, so I went and bought a ticket for the first leg of my trip. I kept checking around me to see if anyone was looking, but nobody seemed to think anything of a fifteen-year-old kid buying a bus ticket. I didn't exactly relax, but now that I was actually here, the fact that I was starving trumped nervousness. The cafeteria was open, so I went in and ordered bacon and eggs, toast, hash browns, *and* pancakes, with a large orange juice. Like I said, I was starving. Outside the window, I couldn't help noticing a billboard for the ZZ Top concert. I had been thinking of going to it with Brian if our parents would let us. It was the weirdest feeling to realize that now that wouldn't happen. It seemed from someone else's life already.

Breakfast was almost eleven dollars. Like I said, I was *starving*. Luckily, it was a cafeteria, so I didn't have to leave a tip. I hated to be chintzy, but I had to watch my bucks. I had almost completely cleaned out my bank account for just about a hundred and seventy dollars—I left twenty in the account so it wouldn't seem too suspicious—and I borrowed a hundred from Brian, making two-seventy total, promising to pay it back as soon as I could. The hundred and seventy plus ten of Brian's money added up to the bus tickets, but I would need to eat and there might be other expenses. I figured the other ninety I had would cover three days if everything went according to plan, so that didn't leave me more than ten dollars a meal, with not much for emergencies. So spending eleven on my first breakfast was kind of dumb, but what can I say, I was *starving*!

I sat in the waiting room, waiting for the bus to be called, still looking around to see if I'd been noticed, but no one seemed to be paying any attention to me. My nervous looking around would probably bring more stares than acting normal would, but then, when I tried to act normal, I couldn't remember how. I kept reminding myself, why should they take any notice of an ordinary kid getting on a bus? After all, I could just be going to Tulsa to visit my sister, for all they knew.

"Now boarding for Sherman, McAlester, Tulsa, and connections beyond," the loudspeaker crackled. My stomach did a back flip. I wasn't quite so sure about that pancake decision all of a sudden. "Platform 6, now boarding." This was it, then. Get on that bus and forever change my life. Turn and go home and forever wonder. There really was no question. I got up and walked out to the platforms, shaking. There were even more diesel fumes and I felt like I was choking. The driver punched my ticket and I climbed into the air-conditioning of the bus.

I threw my knapsack up on the luggage rack, and took a window seat about midway down the bus, in the most anonymous-looking seat I could find. I really hoped I wouldn't end up with a seatmate, and I tried to make myself seem as large as possible—not that that was so large (you might describe me as wiry)—so no one would want to sit next to me. But a lot of people seemed to be headed for Tulsa, and it wasn't long before a kind of young woman with a round face was shoving a bag into the luggage rack and wedging herself in beside me.

"Hi," she said, in a friendly way.

"Hi." I tried to sound sullen. People always seem to be scared of teenagers, so I hoped I could put her off. I was wearing my Rangers cap, and I tried to let the peak of it obscure my face.

"Where y'all goin'?"

"Tulsa." Well, it was true, as far as it went.

"Ooh! I'm headed there, too. Goin' to visit my sister. She just had a baby. I can't wait to see her, the precious thing. My name's Marilu, what's yours?"

"Uh ..." Can't tell her my name. What if the cops are already after me? "Brian." It was the first name I could think of. I hadn't really thought about the fact that I would need aliases and alibis. That I would need to lie.

"What'cha goin' to Tulsa for?" asked Marilu.

The bus door said, "Hush."

"I'm ... uh ... visiting my sister, too."

"She have any babies? I just love babies."

The driver glunked the bus into gear.

"No ... uh ... Christine isn't married. She's ... she's a nurse there, in the hospital." I was scrambling to put together a believable story. So I got Christine from my own name, and the nurse from the nurse I'd seen on the local bus that morning. I figured that to make something convincing, it had to have a couple of little personal details in it. Just state something flat and it sounds funny. People always put in some personal detail when they're telling you something.

"Oh, you're kidding!" Marilu pretty much shrieked. "What a coincidence!"

A little lurch of the bus (and my stomach) and we were moving, the bus wheels were rolling. The skin on my arms prickled.

"Coincidence?" Her sister wasn't a nurse, too, was she? What if she asked a bunch of questions? I was really getting nervous.

"Your sister works in the hospital and mine just had a baby in the hospital!"

I almost laughed with relief. "Yeah. Yeah, I guess you're right. Maybe they met each other."

I was on my way out of Dallas. *Just keep talking to Marilu. Don't think.*

"Is your sister in obstetrics?" quizzed Marilu.

"Obs ... uh, I think she's in a bunch of things." I hoped like mad that this word meant a department or something like that. "I think they move them around."

"Yeah, probably. I wonder if they know each other, though, I mean, both living in Tulsa and all."

"I don't know. It's pretty big, I think."

"Still, though. What's her name?"

"Christine Ramsay." Damn. Why did I practically just give out my own name? When people started looking for me, she'd remember. Damn! "That's her married name, I mean." I tried to fudge it.

"I thought you said she wasn't married."

Oh, brother, what an amateur. "No, she's not," I scrambled. "Not any more. I mean ... she's divorced, you know. She just didn't change her name back yet."

"A lot of people don't bother ... too much trouble. I had this friend who got married real young, and they split up, and then she got married to this other guy—what a creep *he* was—and then she divorced him, and, honest to goodness, I had no idea *what* her name was after all that."

Okay. It was okay. I laughed politely and let her keep talking. As long as she talked, I didn't have to, just nod, smile, ask a question. Some of the time she read a magazine and I gazed out the window. The bus stopped briefly in Richardson, on the north side of the city, for no apparent reason. Soon, the Dallas suburbs slipped away behind

us as we drove along. The fields were thick with bluebon-
nets—it's our state flower, and no wonder—they were like
a sea around us. The sky was like a blue bowl over us, not
one cloud spoiling the blueness. Sometimes a herd of
cows, black and white or brown, or a red barn, broke up
the blueness, or an oil pump bobbed in the distance like
some prehistoric bird. I felt exhilarated. I had done it. I
had escaped, the first step of my trip. I had literally disappeared into the blue.

The bus drove on, through little towns like McKinney
and Sherman. I had come this way before. Ironically, it was
the route we took when I really *had* gone camping with
Brian. The bus stopped at the Sherman Feed and Grain
store (was there any more to Sherman than the Feed and
Grain huge red and white letters?) to pick up a passenger,
and then went on, past the turnoff for the Dwight Eisen-
hower Birthplace, which Brian's parents had once taken
us to—much to our ten-year-old boredom—and then that
was the end of Texas and we were in Oklahoma. Not that
I would have known if I hadn't seen the sign. Oklahoma
looked a lot like Texas. At Durant, the bus passed the turnoff for Lake Texoma State Park. I couldn't help smiling,
remembering when Brian and I had first gone camping
there, when we were eight or nine, and we figured out that
Texoma was half Texas and half Oklahoma. We thought we
were so clever, working that out, and we made up names
for other lakes that could be on state lines—Oklasas, Ten-
tucky, Montaho. Washing-gon and Wyaska were the ones
that really broke us up. We'd whispered new ones to each

other all night in the tent. The best ones, the ones that cracked us up the most, were the state lines that didn't exist: Pennsylsippi, Massakota, Hawazona. How strange that I was out here, alone, on my way to strange states—and I was never going to go back.

Stringtown barely existed. Kiowa was a little more substantial. The bus stopped in a place that didn't even seem to *be* a place called McAlester (Feed and Grain), to let people switch to a local bus for Muskogee, like in that old song, "I'm proud to be an Okie from Muskogee, a place where even squares can have a ball." The houses along the route were crummier than around Dallas. Porches sagged. Curtains hung limp in the windows. Kids looked like they were all in hand-me-downs. It seemed like every second building was a fast-food outlet. Mary Brown's Chicken. Taco Bell. Long John Silver. Did these people eat there? No wonder they were poor if they spent all their money on junk food. I was farther away from home than I'd ever been in my life, or at least since I got to Dallas when I was three. Pretty boring. Pretty flat. Bushes along the side of the road here and there. Henryetta (Feed and Grain). Okmulgee was big enough to have a Wal-mart. Some of the towns' names looked as odd to me as our made-up state lines would've. It was nearly noon when I could see the tallish buildings in Tulsa looming over the prairie horizon. Not Dallas-sized, but still tall.

"Is your sister coming to meet you?" Marilu was asking.

"Uh, no, no, she's at work right now."

"Oh! Then we'll give you a ride. Y'all going to her house?"

"Oh, gee, that's real nice of you. But no, thanks, she said to wait for her at the station."

"Call her."

"I don't have her work number."

"Oh, but you'll be lonely. Bus stations are so nasty."

I smiled, trying to look like I was being brave. This faking it was getting easier. "I'll be fine—really. Anyway, I don't know her exact address for you to take me to." She couldn't argue with that. "You just go on and see your little niece."

"Well, all right," said Marilu, though she seemed disappointed as the bus hauled into the station. She peered across me out the window. "Oh, my gosh, there they are! You wouldn't think they'd bring a precious baby to a nasty old bus station. Oh, look how tiny she is!"

And so on. I let Marilu rush off to the niece while I hung back. The heat had come up and it hit me as I left the air-conditioning. Straight into the Greyhound station, a mini version of the Dallas one. Same signs, same cafeteria. In spite of my huge breakfast, I was starving again. I decided to see what I could afford.

Well, it *was* lunchtime.

I was leaving Tulsa. It was my second bus of the day, and the second time I was sitting beside a youngish woman, but this was a different kind from the last one. She looked smart. Wire glasses with sharp hazel eyes behind them. Straight, shy, light brown hair. Not much of a smile, just a polite, tight-lipped nod as she sat down, and then she pulled out a huge, densely-printed book and a pencil and began to read. She reminded me of Jodie Foster from *Silence of the Lambs* (it was rated R, but Brian and I had managed to get hold of the video when it came out). Now and then, she made a little note in spidery handwriting in the margin. I was grateful I didn't have to introduce myself, explain myself, justify myself. I could just sit back and watch the scenery.

It had been a bit hilly through the middle of Oklahoma but now it was flat again. The further I got away from Dallas, the better I felt. Even if someone had noticed or guessed that I had bought a ticket to Tulsa, from there I could have gone anywhere. It was slightly less likely that they could figure out I was going to St. Louis. There were lots of signs to camping areas, and I kept catching glimpses of water in the distance. It made me think of the times I actually *had* gone camping with Brian and his dad and, again, I had that realization that I was further away from home than I'd ever been in my life since we moved to Dallas. I pictured a miniature bus, with me inside, driving across my map-topped Formica desk. It was a funny feeling, not good or bad, just different. I took a deep breath and laid my head back against the headrest and drifted off to sleep.

It was the first time I'd really slept since I had gotten up Friday morning, and it was warm, soothing, alone, without any dreams that I could remember. Then the bus lurched and I woke up sharply. For a second, I had no idea where I was. On a bus. Going where? Oh, yeah.

The girl beside me was looking at me with an amused expression on her face. What?

"What were you dreaming about?" she asked me.

I didn't think I had been dreaming, until she asked, and then the last little corner of the dream flitted out of my mind. Whatever it was, it was gone. "I don't remember." I stretched my arms. "Nothing, I guess. Why? Did I do something dumb?"

She shook her head. "I'm Beatrice O'Malley," the girl said and offered her hand, so I shook it. It was a little awkward in the cramped bus seat. "I'm a freshman at Tulsa U., and we just learned in psych about R.E.M.s. You had them."

"The band?" I asked, though that didn't make sense.

Beatrice smiled. "No, though I think the band is named after them. Rapid Eye Movements. Everyone gets them when they're dreaming. You were. You have to dream when you go to sleep or you'd go insane."

That was interesting. "Why?"

"I don't know—we haven't taken that yet."

"I'm Paul." This time I borrowed my name from Paula.

"I'm going to Chicago," Beatrice announced, then added, smiling a little smugly, "To see my dad."

"Oh, yeah?"

"I haven't seen him in a while. He works for the government."

"Oh," I said. What was he, a spy? Maybe he was FBI. I'd better be careful.

"Oh, I'm sure you think it's the classic thing—it's in all the movies and everything. Poor little rich girl whose daddy has money but never time for her. But it's not like that at all. My dad and I get along great."

"Great," I said, hoping she'd chatter on like Marilu had so I wouldn't have to answer any hard questions. I thought briefly of my own father. Did I get along with him? I didn't really know. "Get along" wasn't really what it was about with my dad. That was really all we did—get along. We got out of Monday and along into Tuesday, and out of Tuesday and along into Wednesday.

"I mean, we don't have to say a lot, but we both know we love each other," Beatrice was saying. I was thinking that my dad and I never said we loved each other, but that was just a normal guy thing, right? "Of course, ever since

my parents got divorced, I haven't seen him as much ...
but listen to me rattle on. What about you? Where're you
headed?"

"Me? Oh, just up to St. Louis. My older sister fell and hurt
her leg, and I'm just going to stay with her a little while,
help her out around the house, you know, mowing the
lawn and stuff." Geez. Where was this stuff coming from?

"What about school? Won't you miss school?"

Yikes! "Oh, yeah ... uh ... I got special permission. I'll finish my year doing correspondence."

"Wow," Beatrice replied quietly. "That's a lot of work.
You're a really nice brother. I sometimes wish I had a
brother. I'm an only child."

"Me, too," I replied comfortably, then gulped, almost
like the cartoons, when I realized what I had said. I
hoped she didn't notice, but Beatrice looked at me
sharply. Uh-oh. "I mean, I grew up as an only child. My
sister's way older, she's like forty ..." Too old, too old! "...
or thirty-five or something."

Beatrice was still looking at me, but changed the sub-
ject. "So, what college are going to go to?"

Whew.

"Oh, I don't know, it's a couple of years away yet." College? I didn't even know where I was going tomorrow.

"But you are going to college?"

"Yeah, I hope so. I don't know, somewhere local, I guess."

"Go to Tulsa U. You're what, a sophomore?" I nodded.
"So, by the time you're frosh at Tulsa, I'll still be there, a
senior. I'll show you around."

It was a nice picture, in a way, if any of it had anything to do with reality. I smiled.

"You *are* from Tulsa, aren't you?" Beatrice was asking me. "I never asked you."

"Oh, yeah, yeah. Well. Just outside." I cast back in my mind for the last exit sign I could remember seeing on the way into town. "Uh ... Beggs."

Beatrice nodded slowly. "What will you major in, do you think? I mean ..." she put on a funny voice "... 'What do you wanna be when you grow up?' like they always ask you."

I grinned. "A baseball player. A bass player—not that I know any music. A bass fisher. A basket weaver. I don't know."

"A poet," said Beatrice, and smiled back. "Or a novelist— lots of chance to make up stories."

Yikes again. What did she mean? "What do you mean?" I asked, trying to sound casual.

"I just think you have a good imagination," she said, just as casual.

"You don't even know me, though ..." I started, then decided I should let this line of conversation drop.

"No, I don't," agreed Beatrice. "Do I, Paul?" She was smiling a little at me now.

I turned and gazed out the window. The countryside was a little more rolling and there were more trees than before. There were signs like *Ozark Autobody*, so I supposed we were in or near the Ozark Mountains, probably into Missouri by now. It wasn't really mountainous, though. A lot like Texas. Cirrus clouds were streaking across the sky and occasionally cast shadows as we rode on. I could see Beatrice's reflection in the window. She was still looking at me, or rather at my reflection. She wasn't smiling now. She knew I was lying, I could just tell. The vibration of the bus and the imperfection of the glass made her seem to hover, unreal, outside the bus. But she was real inside the bus. I turned back to the real Beatrice.

"It's okay, I shouldn't have said anything," she said. "I'm sorry."

"How did you know?" I wondered what she did know.

"You were working too hard at your story. Too concerned about the details. You 'doth protest too much,' like they say."

"Hm," I said, then thought of something. "Like you."

"Me? Hey, I'm the psych major here. About what?"

"Your dad. You get along great."

"Okay, we're even. I wish I had brothers and sisters and stuff. More family."

"Me, too," I said, and we both smiled at each other for a moment. It felt nice, right. I'm not a liar at heart.

Beatrice broke the connection, looked down. "I mean, you don't have to tell me, but, well, where are you going really?"

Damn. I looked at the back of the seat in front of me. I wanted to tell her the truth, she seemed so nice, but did I dare trust her? She was a psychology major, maybe wanted to be a social worker or something. She might want to "rescue" me. She might tell. And then there was her dad, the spy for the FBI.

"It's okay," Beatrice said, shaking her head. "Sorry I asked." She turned back to her book.

I felt awful as the bus rolled on. She was nice! We were getting into the suburbs of St. Louis now. There were quite a lot more trees and they were bigger. I wasn't *trying* to be mean. The land was flatter again and more built-up with houses and stores and warehouses, and the highways were wider. I didn't have a choice. I gazed hard out the window to avoid having to deal with her. It was funny how I hadn't minded lying to her before, but now it upset me that I couldn't tell her anything. Almost all the buildings were made of brick. I didn't know what to do with my hands.

E ven though it was Saturday, the traffic into St. Louis was heavy. I actually felt kind of excited when I saw a turnoff to Memphis. I thought I saw a glint of water and figured it must be the Mississippi. The very name of that great river is romantic. I was surprised to see how brown the water was. It all made me think of Huckleberry Finn, and that made me grin a little to myself. Here I was, Chris Ramsay, off on an adventure, kind of like Huckleberry Finn. Except that Huck just lit out. I was going somewhere. And except for Beatrice, no one on this planet knew where I was. And she didn't know *who* I was. I had never before felt so grown-up.

From the window I could see the famous arch that looks like a giant-sized half-McDonald's. Beside the highway was a huge wreck of a building called Powell Square. It was kind of a weird and interesting thing to see. From the highway, I could see Busch Memorial Stadium, where Bob Tewkesbury was starting out pitching what looked like it was going to be a winning season. Maybe he was even in there, warming up right now, for all I knew.

We soon pulled into a large and busy bus station. As the bus came to a halt, I glanced over at Beatrice, who was stuffing her textbook into her backpack. I couldn't just leave it like that.

"It was nice meeting you," I said, feeling strangely shy.

She looked at me, startled. "Likewise," she replied, and hurried off the bus. I felt disappointed, disappointing. But what else could I have done?

I slung my pack over my right shoulder and took off my Rangers ball cap, shoving it into the pocket of my jean jacket. No point in advertising I was from Texas. I knew that, in theory, I had until late Sunday afternoon before the alarm was raised that I was missing. But I had no way of knowing whether my plan had worked. Maybe they were already out looking for me.

I walked into the bus station to pay my fare on to Indianapolis but, as I headed for the ticket counter, I pulled up sharp. There were two cops at the counter, showing the clerk something that looked like a photo. Were they already on to me?

I told myself to keep calm, but my heart was pounding and my mouth went dry. Maybe it was nothing. Maybe it was some other kid. But what if they were already looking for me? The clerk was shaking his head, for the time being. But if I went up to buy a ticket right now, the ticket seller would certainly recognize me from the picture he'd seen only seconds earlier.

I headed for the men's room to stop and think, going into one of the cubicles for privacy.

All right, here were the things. I was hungry and wanted some dinner. I needed to get a ticket to Indianapolis. But I couldn't buy it from that particular ticket seller, just in case. Could I wait till the seller went off shift or on break? Maybe, but I might miss the bus and I couldn't afford to waste time waiting for the next one, whenever that would be. I knew I had a couple of hours before I had to buy the ticket. Finally, I decided to go to the coffee shop—I could see the ticket window from there—and grab some dinner at the same time.

I picked up a tray and moved along the cafeteria line.

Another meal in a bus station. I got French fries and a hamburger, with a glass of water because it was free, and chose a table that had a so-so view of the ticket window. I didn't want to be too visible. I also had a so-so view of Beatrice, who was settled in at a table by the window to the outside, sipping a coffee, with her nose still in her book. I ate my burger as slowly as I could and, one by one, nibbled my fries till they got cold. I wondered how long they would let me sit here without buying anything, but no one seemed to notice me.

I wondered how they could even have a picture of me. "Clutter" and all, we didn't have any. We didn't even have a camera at home. Well, that was starting to make sense. And that made me wonder if my dad would actually look for me when he found I was gone, because wouldn't that match up with the *Missing Kids* picture? And then, he'd be the one caught in the lie he'd been feeding me all these years. It made me shiver a little, to realize how everything I believed was true wasn't. It made me hate him a little.

The ticket seller didn't budge. He was one of those old buzzards, in a cardigan and plaid shirt, who did everything at the same speed—dead slow. I was beginning to think he was really some kind of elaborate robot who was never going to leave, when finally a young guy came and spoke to him. I watched. Was the old guy really going to go on break?

The yearbook. There'd be a picture of me from last year. No, wait, I missed picture day—that was the day my dad declared Ditch Day and we were supposed to go to Six

Flags, since there was a new roller-coaster, and I was excited, since we didn't usually do things like that, but then we didn't after all. Oh. Hm. That was starting to make sense. He was keeping my picture out of the yearbook.

But there *was* a picture of me from the track team. But the school would be closed on the weekend, so they couldn't ... unless, somehow, the cops had the school yearbook. Would they do that?

The old guy turned and started to move away from the counter, and the young guy moved into his place. This was it! I started to stand up. Wait. The old guy turned back, started to say something to the young guy. Wait. The young guy nodded, okay. Wait. The old guy opened a drawer and pulled out a piece of paper that looked like a photograph. Damn. I sat back down, hoping no one had noticed me. Damn. Now what was I going to do? Damn. I couldn't buy a ticket from this ticket seller, either.

I looked helplessly around the coffee shop. And then I saw the answer, across the way, settled in at a table by the window to the outside, sipping a coffee, with her nose still in her book. *I* couldn't buy a ticket. But Beatrice could. No one was looking for *her*.

But would she? I stood up, steeled myself, and crossed the coffee shop, stopping at her table. Beatrice looked up.

"Oh!" she said. I didn't blame her for being surprised.

"Look, I know you think I'm a runaway. But I'm not."

Beatrice just looked at me.

"I need your help."

She nodded.

"I'm sorry I lied to you on the bus. I'm sorry I didn't tell you the truth. I just wasn't sure ..."

I sat down opposite her. Even now, I didn't know if I could trust her. She didn't smile, didn't speak. But it was my only shot.

"I'm not running away. I'm running *to*," I explained. "My dad, kind of ... well, it's not so good living with him. I have an aunt in ... Vermont. If I can get to her, it'll be all right. But if my dad catches up with me, I'll never get away." Well, it was as close to the truth as I dared.

"Does your dad ... hit you?"

I looked down at the tabletop. It was white with gold flecks. I hated this. Lying to her again. Drawing on her sympathy. My dad may be a lot of things, but he never hit me.

"Worse?" Her voice dropped to a whisper.

I couldn't answer her suggestion. "I saw cops showing a picture to the ticket seller. It might not have been me, but I can't go up to the counter, just in case. Can you help me? If I give you the money, can you buy my ticket as far as Indianapolis?"

Beatrice was nodding. "I'll buy it all the way to Vermont, if you like," she offered.

I shook my head. "Better not, just in case. They'd know where I'm going, then."

Beatrice looked at me. She knew. I pulled out my wallet and handed the money to her. As I waited for her to come back, I played with the saltshaker, pushed on the napkins in their metal holder and watched them spring back, spun the empty ashtray with my finger. I looked anywhere but at the ticket booth. In a moment, or an eternity (actually, an hour passed accidentally, because I looked at the clock and realized we'd crossed time zones, which was a very weird feeling. I reset my watch), she was back with the ticket.

"The picture's not you."

"How do you know?"

"I saw it on the counter. It's a black girl."

Relief washed through me and I couldn't keep from grinning. "Thanks." I breathed deeply once or twice, hauling coffee smells and grease and gravy and cigarette smoke and diesel exhaust into my lungs. I hadn't even realized how tense I'd been. "Thanks," I said again.

The P.A. system boomed. "Now boarding at berth four for Springfield, Bloomington, Joliet, Chicago." .

"That's my bus," said Beatrice. She grabbed a napkin from the metal dispenser and scribbled something on it. "When you get wherever it is you're going, will you send me a postcard? Just so I won't worry?" She shoved the napkin at me. "That's my address at school." I nodded and folded the napkin into my top jacket pocket, buttoning it shut for safety. "I won't expect to see a Vermont postmark," she added.

I smiled at her. "Have a good time with your dad."

"Thanks. Good luck. Be careful." She grabbed my hand and squeezed it and was gone.

"Thanks," I said again, as she dashed away.

I looked down at the white-with-gold table, feeling a little guilty, but mostly relieved. Beatrice had left her pen on the table. I looked up to call after her but she was gone.

It was only a cheap Bic pen, slightly, but not very, chewed at the top. I wondered what the psych major would have to say about that. I tucked the pen into my backpack and headed for the bus.

I could have had Beatrice buy my ticket right through, but it made me nervous to think anyone, even Beatrice, had the information about where I was headed, so that's why I had only asked her to buy the ticket as far as Indianapolis. I picked my usual anonymous spot on the bus, on the right-hand side about halfway back. I figured it was the best place to be out of the driver's view, not at the front where I could be seen, or at the back where the rabble always sat, and on the side away from the rearview mirror. This time the bus was pretty empty, and I was glad to be sitting alone as I crossed the Mississippi. Lights gleamed in the river below and there were even lit-up paddle wheelers churning along, no doubt for the tourists—it was much more glamorous-looking by night when you couldn't see the famous mud that I had forgotten about. The very river that Mark Twain piloted the paddle wheelers on. The Mississippi!

I had never imagined the river to be so wide, so beautiful, so *dividing*. The Mississippi is the division between the west and the east of America, and here, where we crossed from Missouri into Illinois, it felt to me I was leaving behind one kind of America and moving into another, where the big cities and small cities were. The bridge was like a point of no return. If I had turned back from St. Louis, I would have had time to get back to Dallas before I was missed, likely. But not from Indianapolis.

My head was such a jumble of thoughts, I figured I would be up all night. I pulled a sweatshirt out of my pack to make a pillow. At least I could be comfortable in my confusion. But in no time at all, I guess I was fast asleep.

THE MIDDLE OF NOWHERE: SUNDAY, THE MIDDLE OF THE NIGHT

In the middle of the night—it seemed like we must've been traveling a long time, but really we couldn't have been—I vaguely felt the bus stop, figured it must be Terre Haute. I shifted to get more comfortable and fell back asleep.

A while later, I gradually became aware of the bumping of the bus, and a general lightening of the sky told me that it was morning. I was surprised for a second to be waking up in a bus, but I guess I was getting used to the traveling. When a shaft of light hit me in the face, I opened my eyes. I had been sitting alone when I had left St. Louis. Now there was someone beside me. A man in a uniform. Was this it? Was I being arrested?

But it was a soldier, not a cop. He just grinned and said "Hi" when he saw I was awake.

"Hi." I was wary, still not sure if something was up. "Say, do you know where we are? How far to Indianapolis?"

"You mean, how far *from* Indianapolis. Didja mean to get off there?"

We were past Indianapolis? And I hadn't been thrown off the bus for not having a ticket?

"U-uh, no." I was desperately trying to remember where the bus went next. "Fort Wayne," I hazarded.

"'Bout 'nother hournalf to there."

He still sounded American, but I realized I'd come a

long way. I think he meant an hour and a half. His way of talking was just quick, flatter than I was used to.

"You're a soldier, hunh?"

"No kidding. Private Cam Taylor." Cam saluted, but he was kidding around. "Seen action, too, in the Persian Gulf."

"Yeah? My dad was in Viet Nam." No, he wasn't, you moron. Why are you saying this?

"My dad was in Nam, too," said Cam. "Came back with a busted leg. Hey, it'd be cool if they knew each other. Jim Taylor. He was a sergeant."

"I don't think he ever mentioned him. My dad's name is ... O'Malley, Stu O'Malley ... uh ... Irish Stu, they called him." Hey. That wasn't bad.

"What rank?"

"Private, first class." At least I can say one thing that's true, even if my dad never actually went to Viet Nam. At least, supposing he'd told me the truth about that.

"Where was he stationed?" Cam went on.

"You got me there." I could never have faked that. I fell back on my sister the nurse in Tulsa. "I think he got moved around a lot."

"You from Texas?"

"Yeah."

"Had a buddy in the Gulf from Texas. Man, that guy could eat." Cam shook his head at the memory. "Yep, I'm home on leave for a week. Gonna see my folks and my kid brother and eat my mom's fine apple pie—up in Saginaw. God's country." He smiled dreamily, a big, honest, goofy kind of grin. I wasn't sure if he was thinking of his home town or the apple pie. "Where you headed?"

"Back to school," I sighed.

"What, you're in boarding school?"

"Yeah. Sissy place. They think they're in England or somewhere. They play stuff like soccer, instead of real sports like baseball and football."

"How come you have to go to boarding school?"

"Well ..." Here, I sighed for effect. I had a plan in mind and I was working my way up to it. "My mom died, you know, and my dad, well, he's higher up in the military now, and they've got him over in Europe, and he's always traveling around. But we get along great," I added, a-little-too-enthusiastically-on-purpose. Thank you, Beatrice.

"So, where are you coming from?" asked Cam.

Right. "Oh, I was visiting my sister. She's a nurse in Tulsa." Well, why not? "God, I hate school. So tell me about the Persian Gulf. Was it cool—I mean, obviously not, but, y'know?"

"Cool's hardly the word—it was stinking hot," and Cam launched into a long and somewhat technical discussion of his pivotal role in the entire conflict, which sounded kind of exciting, if not very believable. It was kind of funny, both of us lying to each other, and I wondered whether he was only pretending to believe me, too. Lying about believing a liar. That was something new.

The buildings were getting closer together and the traffic thicker, so I knew we must be getting close to Fort Wayne. Ever since we came into St. Louis, I had noticed that there was just a lot more traffic than there had been. Cam's story was just coming to an end and my next plan was in place.

"What I wouldn't give to live a life like that." I hoped I wasn't too over the top. "I mean, to be out there, really doing something. Instead of being stuck in school."

"It won't be long till you can sign up to the army. That's the life, man. See the world. Really do something, like you said."

"You read my mind." I lowered my voice a little. "Look, I haven't exactly told you the truth about me. I'm going to boarding school all right, but my dad's not in Europe. He was hurt kinda bad in Nam, and he has to use a wheelchair. He's pretty mad about it, and he takes it out on himself and everyone around him. Well, you know what happened to some people in that war."

"Heroin?" asked Cam in a low voice.

I just shrugged. "My mom left some money in trust for me, enough to send me to this school. She picked it because it was near where she was from and far from him. But I hate it. Anyway, what I really want to do is get out of there, join up to the army."

"After what it did to your dad?"

"That wouldn't happen to me. If I got hurt, I'd just pick up my life and go on. But the thing is: I'm not quite eighteen. Well, all right, I'm not quite seventeen. But I just can't stand this sissy school any longer. So I wrote to my cousin, who lives near Toledo, and he said he'd lend me his ID. But I have to get to Toledo to borrow it and sign up. Thing is, the school usually sends someone to pick us up. So, why I'm telling you this is, if I can slip away to the men's room, would you buy me a ticket to Toledo and meet me in there with it? If they don't see me, they'll just figure I'm on the next bus, and then I can come out and head for Toledo."

"Won't they recognize you getting off the bus?"

"Nah, they're so lazy, they always wait in the car in the parking lot." Where on earth was I getting stuff like this from?

There was a pause while Cam considered. *Come on, come on.* Beatrice did it for me. If you do it, too, I'll be so far from where I bought my last ticket that no one will have a clue where I've gone if they try to track me. *Come on, come on.*

"Sure, kid," said Cam finally. "I'm a little nervous about you going into the army so young and all, but, well, I think you'll be all right."

Yes! "Oh, thanks, man." The bus was pulling into the Fort Wayne bus terminal. I took out my wallet and gave Cam a fifty. Bonus to get Cam to break the fifty so no one would notice me doing it. "That should cover it. Thanks, man!" I shook Cam's hand.

We swung off the bus and didn't speak, as though we didn't know each other. Nobody challenged me for my ticket, which kind of surprised me, but I figured bus ticket fraud maybe isn't a widespread crime. I supposed it was technically stealing, not to pay for the trip from Indianapolis to Fort Wayne, but I thought, well, the bus was going anyway, and I didn't add much weight to the load. Besides, if I tried to do something about it, I'd only call attention to myself and, on top of that, it was a stroke of luck to save that money, and I figure if you're having some luck, you don't mess around with it.

I was ready for breakfast but I headed straight to the men's room to wait for Cam. One glance in the mirror and I decided to clean myself up a bit while I was waiting. I really was a mess. My hair was flat and dull looking—it was Sunday morning and I hadn't had a shower since Friday morning, hadn't brushed my teeth since yesterday morning. In spite of the heavy sleep I'd had on the St. Louis to Indianapolis ride (and a little beyond), it wasn't a long sleep and my eyes looked dull and red. I was starting to get the slightest stubble, though it didn't show much since my hair was light and I wasn't yet up to shaving every day. Although I looked awful, I also thought I looked kind of cool, kind of road-weary, kind of like something out of a book or—kind of—Kurt Cobain, from Nirvana. I thought I looked lean, and tough, and maybe a little bit older than I had just twenty-four hours ago.

When my teeth were brushed and my face was a bit cleaner—I didn't even try to deal with the dirt under my fingernails—I started to think it was about time Cam turned up. Probably there was a line at the ticket counter— I hadn't noticed.

A few more minutes had ticked by when I had a sudden sickening thought. What if Cam had decided to turn me in and was right now outside the bus station looking for some driver from some fancy school? It wouldn't take him long to figure out there wasn't one and that I was a runaway, and he'd go to the cops, and here I was, a sitting duck in the men's room with only one door in or out. After all, the guy was a soldier—probably a pretty by-the-book kind of guy, now that I thought about it.

I shoved my toothbrush back into the pack and moved toward the door. Maybe there was still time. Or maybe I'd open the door and walk into the welcoming long arms of the law. Well, I couldn't live in the men's room of the Fort Wayne bus terminal, so I'd have to risk it. The longer I waited, the worse my chances were.

I steeled myself and began to reach for the door handle. Suddenly, the door burst open. I jumped back. Some guy brushed past me.

"Sorry, man," the guy muttered distractedly as the door slammed back.

In the moment the door had been open, I hadn't noticed any posse waiting there, noose at the ready for me, so I opened the door and went out.

The waiting room wasn't very big and it wasn't very busy. I could see in one glance that Cam wasn't there. I decided to risk going over to the ticket counter.

"Excuse me," I said. "Could you tell me where the men's rooms are?"

"Right behind you," said the ticket seller, not looking up.

"Is that the only one?" Maybe Cam was waiting for me somewhere else.

Now the ticket seller looked up with a strange expression on his face. "Yeah," he replied. "Why? Something wrong with it?"

"No, no, I just—" I just stopped talking and wandered away. I couldn't think of anything logical to say, anyway.

I dropped down on a bench, feeling lousy. What was Cam up to? Was I in danger of being caught, sitting out in the open like this?

"Last call for local bus to Lansing, Flint, Saginaw, Bay City, and Midland, platform three," came the voice over the loudspeaker.

And then I knew. I grabbed my pack and ran outside. By the time I got to platform three, the bus was pulling out.

Cam saw me from its window and, as the bus turned out onto the road, he waved at me. With a fifty-dollar bill.

Fifty dollars gone. I felt like I'd been punched in the stomach, not just because of the money, but because I'd trusted that skunk. Then again, I'd only lied to him myself. Well, there was no use in wallowing—I had to figure out what to do. Across the street was a McDonald's and I headed there to get some breakfast. At least it would be cheaper than the bus station, probably.

Sitting in a corner by the window, forking back hash browns, not because I wanted them but because it was the cheapest thing they had, I tried to think what to do next. My mind kept going back to the fifty and I could hardly swallow the food, even though I was starving. If only I hadn't fallen asleep on the bus from St. Louis. Then I probably wouldn't even have met that jerk. And I wouldn't have stolen that ride to Fort Wayne. That was what did it; that was what turned my luck. It wasn't the lies I'd been telling; they were necessary and, anyway, they didn't hurt anyone. But stealing was different. Wasn't it? I'd always been taught both were wrong. By my dad—the biggest liar and thief on earth. My stomach turned to lead again when I thought of the total deception my life was based on until two days ago. It was ...

No. I didn't have time to wallow in that now. I pulled my thoughts back to the problems right in front of me. I counted my money. After paying for breakfast, I had about eighty-five dollars left. And crossing the border had now become urgent. It was about nine o'clock and my dad would be expecting me home by three or four. Make that five my time since crossing into the Eastern Time Zone just before Indianapolis. And it was over one hundred and fifty miles to Detroit still.

The only bright spot was that at least Cam probably wouldn't turn me in, since he turned out to be a thief, too.

Somehow, taking the bus didn't seem like a good idea any more. Mainly because, if I had to pay for tickets, I couldn't have anything to eat, and I still probably had a day or more traveling beyond today. It looked like the only thing for it was to hitchhike.

A transit map I picked up a few minutes later, from a spinner rack back in the bus terminal, showed me how to get to the highway, and soon I was standing on the side of Highway 24, hitching a ride to Toledo. Oh, of course I knew it wasn't a good idea, but what choice did I have?

I was surprised when one of the first cars stopped for me. It was a white Lincoln. I ran ahead to where the car was stopped and I opened the door. Very plush.

"Where ya headed?" asked the driver, a balding, middle-aged man. It seemed okay—what did I know?—so I jumped in.

"Toledo."

"Oh, too bad. I'm headed for Columbus—I won't be able

to take you far. Just to New Haven, where the road splits."

"That's okay." Better than nothing. And I buckled my seatbelt as the Lincoln edged out onto the almost empty road.

"Yessir, I'm headed down to Columbus. Sales conference. I'm a commercial traveler. You can talk about your information super-highway all you like, but nothing will ever beat the personal touch. I'll tell you, that's where the coin will always be. As you can see." He indicated the car.

The car certainly was comfortable. As the salesman launched into a discussion of why IBM was the wave of the future—probably his sales pitch—I settled back into the plush red seat. "Twenty years from now, kids'll be asking, 'Daddy, what was Apple?'" Tall white puffy clouds floated above us, but mostly the sun was out and it was cozy and comfortable in the car.

Next thing I knew, the car's tires were pulling onto gravel, and I woke up in time to hear the salesman saying, "Well, I'm sorry I can't take you any further, you've been great company. I always pick up hitchhikers. You know, in spite of what they say, it's great to have company on the road. You just get so tired of hearing your own voice rattling around in your brain, you know. Anyway, young fella, you take care now, and don't take any wooden nickels."

I resurfaced from the car and thanked the driver, and suddenly, I was all alone on a fork in the road just a few miles outside of Fort Wayne.

After half an hour of waiting for another ride, I was beginning to regret that I had taken the ride from the salesman. There were a lot fewer cars out here, and the few there were didn't stop. On the other hand, this was the way to Toledo, so if they weren't coming from Fort Wayne, they wouldn't have been back in Fort Wayne, either, if I'd stayed there. I also didn't like the look of the sky very much. It was still mostly sunny, but there were a lot more clouds than there had been before. And if I didn't cross the border by this afternoon—well, there just was no other option—I had to. I wondered vaguely if I should have had a passport, but it was just Canada, so probably not. I had my school ID. Still, though. That could be enough to tell them that "MC Missing Chris" was "in da house." Well, maybe they wouldn't ask. (Or maybe I wasn't "Missing Chris" yet—that was my best chance.) It would be different if it was Mexico, but I thought Canada was sort of—well, not part of the U.S., obviously, but kind of like a cousin. Not that I knew what that meant, really.

I tried to imagine what my father would do when he discovered I was missing. Would he have any idea at all that I was heading for my mother? I thought that my father might be paranoid about that very thing happening—or even of my mother finding me and kidnapping me back. But it was hard to know how he would react. Would he want to involve the cops right away? Would he maybe just take off himself, figuring the jig was up? Or would he assume that he was clever enough that he'd never get caught and think that I'd run away for some other reason? He could think something had happened to me. But probably not, since I had said I would be away, and the first thing Brian's dad would say was that I hadn't been camping with them. My father would know something was up then. I never should have taken that Santa picture; he could have noticed by now, and that was a dead giveaway where I was headed. It was just impossible to imagine what was going on in Dallas, so I gave up driving myself nuts.

Slowly, another car approached, first as a dot on the horizon that could take either road. Take the left fork, I willed it, take the left fork. The car took the left fork, and I stood up and stuck my thumb out, trying to look wholesome. The rusted silver Bel Air slowly approached and came to a stop.

I pulled open the door.

"Hop in, son," invited the driver, a middle-aged man, a black man with grizzled salt-and-pepper hair. He didn't look like a pervert. Then again, how would I know what a pervert looked like? I took a deep breath and hopped in.

"Where you headed, son?" the man asked.

"Toledo," I replied, hoping the guy would say he was going all the way to Detroit.

"Well, I'm only headed as far as Defiance today, son,
but that'll put you on your way. Name's Walker. Reverend
Sherman Walker. I thank the good Lord He has brought us
together." The Reverend Sherman Walker offered me his
hand. I took it and Mr. Walker closed his other hand over
mine. It should have been weird but it wasn't; it was nice. I
felt like I was literally in good hands. "It is part of His divine
plan," Walker finished up, letting go of my hand and putting the car into gear.

"Now, what, may I ask, is your name, son?"

I really wanted to tell him the truth, he seemed like such
a good guy, and especially since he was a preacher. Somehow, it seemed *really* wrong to lie to a guy with a direct
line to God. But this was exactly the guy not to tell, because
he'd for sure turn me in. I couldn't look directly at him and
glanced down at the floor. There was a penny on the floor
mat, lying heads up. I was grateful it wasn't George "I can-
not tell a lie" Washington gazing up at me.

"Lincoln," I started lying. Honest Abe. Just as bad. "Lincoln Taylor." Damn. Why did I invoke the name of that
thief, Cam Taylor? An honest man plus a crook. Seemed
like as good a name as any just at the moment. Oh well, it
was only for about forty miles, according to the sign we'd
just passed.

"And Lincoln, on what business has the Lord seen fit to
call you to Toledo by such unconventional means?"

"Oh ... uh." I had concocted a story about being left

behind by friends, but since it involved me having been drunk, it didn't seem appropriate now. "My sister lives there. I've been having some trouble at home with my dad, and she said I could come stay with her, but I didn't have enough money for the bus." Well, that was as close as I'd come yet to the truth. Mr. Walker glanced over at me and the car swerved a little over the white line. Fortunately, there was nothing coming.

"Your sister is very kind to you. What sort of trouble is it that you and your father can't work out?"

"It's just ... he's always telling me what to do, where to be, how to think. He won't let me grow up and be me."

"Have you had angry words between you?" Mr. Walker looked searchingly at me. I looked out the windshield and noticed that again we'd swerved over the line.

"Hey, be careful!"

"The Lord will take care of us," replied the Reverend Sherman Walker, pulling the car back into its lane.

I could only hope Mr. Walker had said his prayers that morning, because it didn't look much like anybody but the Lord was going to be taking care of us.

"What is the nature of your trouble?" Mr. Walker was asking.

"Oh, mostly I just do what he says, but it makes me mad. I feel like I'm inside a box that's smaller than me." Mr. Walker was quiet. "The thing that makes me maddest, though, is that I can never stand up to him, I can never say, 'Stop this, Dad, let me be me.' Like on Tuesday, when I made Minute Rice instead of potatoes for dinner. And he doesn't, you know, *say* anything, he just fixes you with this *look* and I just *cave*."

Suddenly, I realized that I was telling this man the truth about my life. Better be careful.

"And what about your mother? Where is she in all this?"

I looked out the window at the cows in the fields. "My mom died when I was three." This lie, at least, was easy to tell. I'd believed it myself until Wednesday.

"Then I know your mother's spirit is watching down from heaven, keeping you safe from harm. How does your father feel about you going to stay with your blessed sister?"

"Tell you the truth? I think he's kind of relieved I'm leaving. I think I'm just a trouble to him. Like ... like a dog who won't heel or stay when you tell him to." I thought of Rover, who just sat there with a dog's version of a goofy grin on his face, like he was permanently saying, "Let's play frisbee!" and how it annoyed my dad. And I thought of how close to the truth I had come with this man up to now, and wondered if maybe there was even some truth to this, too. It was a new thought, and I would have to think about it some more, because it didn't seem to make any sense— why had he stolen me if he didn't really want me? And yet it did. It did make sense.

"Your mother's spirit. That's why your sister has taken you in, and that's why the Lord has allowed me to spend this time with you today. 'The Lord works in mysterious ways His wonders to perform,' son. You needed to talk about your father to a stranger—your sister will have her own perspective. Just as the Lord forgives us our sins, I know in time you will find it in your heart to forgive your father."

Maybe. As Mr. Walker went on about pain, forgiveness, and the holy mercy of God, I half listened. What he was saying didn't seem really to apply to me or to the fake me, either, so I took some time to do some mental arithmetic. As far as I could figure it, without actually taking out my map, I thought that even after this guy let me off in Defiance, I still had a hundred, a hundred and twenty-five miles to go to the border at Detroit. Now, even if I had a car of my own, (or a license, for that matter) that would be at least a couple of hours, which put me in Canada (if I was *lucky*) in mid-afternoon. And I was due home in Dallas around three or four. I wondered how long my dad would wait before calling up Brian's house to see if we were back. And I wondered again what my dad would actually *do* when he figured out that I was gone. How soon would the alarm be put out—if it were put out? It was already Sunday morning.

Sunday morning? I kind of didn't want to know the answer but, still, I was curious. I waited for a convenient jumping-in break in Mr. Walker's mini-sermon and asked, "Say, Reverend Walker, if you're a reverend, how come you're not in church on Sunday morning? Shouldn't you be preaching somewhere?"

"Well, I am preaching. I'm preaching right here and now," replied the driver, swerving again into the next lane. Luckily, the highway was nearly deserted. I looked around for a St. Christopher medal or something, but it looked like Mr. Walker was of a Christian persuasion that didn't go in for saints.

Strange thoughts began slipping into my head, taking up posts like silent sentries, and I started feeling in the front pocket of my pack for Beatrice's pen, just in case. The pen is mightier than the sword, they say. Maybe it could even *be* a sword, Beatrice. Or, at least a dagger, if necessary.

"You know, I may not be a preacher in the eyes of the church anymore," he went on, "but I'm still a preacher in the eyes of the Lord."

Yikes. I wondered why he was no longer a preacher, but I didn't dare ask. I clutched the pen in my fist, point out.

"Not all His good works are done from the pulpit, Lincoln." Walker smiled, but I almost thought his smile looked like a leer. Every cautionary tale I'd ever heard about the dangers of hitchhiking marched through my head now. The car's right wheels hit the gravel at the side of the road. Was this just Walker's usual swerving, or was he stopping the car? I was sure the car was slowing and soon both sets of wheels were off the road, and the car was coming to a stop. Walker reached back into a bag in the back seat. What now?

Mr. Walker was holding a beautiful, shiny apple out to me. Now the stories of Halloween razor blades and Snow White and the warnings about taking candy from strangers flared up in my mind. And, hey, while we're on the biblical theme, how about Adam and Eve and the Garden of Eden? What strange temptation was this supposed to be?

"We have now come to the end of our journey together," said Walker, while I tried to find the door handle behind my back with my left hand, still gripping Beatrice's pen with my right. "We are in Defiance. Did you know that this was where Johnny Appleseed had his nursery? It was here that he raised his apples and gathered the seeds he took, with the Word of God, to communities throughout America."

Johnny Appleseed? I shook my head.

"It is here that I come to refresh my commitment to the Lord, so that *I* may continue his good work and spread the Word. Your company has done me a power of good. Hearing your story has helped me with my own.

Please accept an apple as a small token of my gratitude."

My head was exploding. This whole ride had taken a very unexpected turn. Still thinking of poison and razor blades, I took the apple and managed to say thanks.

Suddenly, Walker threw his head back and, in a very nice voice he sang out, "Ohhh! The Lord is good to me / And so I thank the Lord / For giving me the things I need / The sun and the rain and the apple seed / The Lord is good to me."

I finally found the handle and was out of the car. "Thanks for the ride!"

As I closed the door, Walker called after me, "The peace of Jesus Christ be upon you and your family." The Bel Air pulled away, spraying me with gravel, and turned off at the exit a hundred yards or so ahead.

I loosened my grip on the pen and looked carefully at the apple. There didn't seem to be any razor slits in it, but I put it in my pack. No point in getting poisoned. I'd wash the apple before I ate it, if I ate it at all. I was in the middle of nowhere without a car in sight. Clouds were piling up seriously in the western sky.

It was nice at least to feel a little cooler, because there wasn't much shade where Walker had dropped me off. I was sitting perched on my rolled-up sleeping bag, munching on one of Paula's chocolate bars and wondering how I was going to get through Toledo. The map showed I had about sixty miles to get there, and then another sixty on to Detroit. But unless I was dead lucky, I wasn't likely to get a ride through Toledo, and it was all ringed with expressways where I wouldn't likely have much luck getting a ride and might get picked up by the cops. I might be able to get through town on local transit, but I had no idea how to do that, and I was a little nervous about asking too many questions, especially as I was definitely looking grubbier by the minute.

And then there was the matter of getting to Toledo at all. As each car appeared in the distance, I stood to thumb a ride, but no one stopped for about three-quarters of an hour. My unease was rising toward panic. Finally, an oldish brown Dodge van pulled up.

"Hey, hop in, man," invited the guy in the passenger

seat, leaning forward to let me into the back. The music was blaring full blast.

I climbed into the van and flopped into a back seat. Including the driver and the guy who had spoken to me, there were four guys in the car, all around twenty years old, all rocker types. The music in the van came from a boom box. It was Metallica. All right! All four guys had long hair, and one had on purple vinyl pants and royal blue leather boots. The air was thick with cigarette smoke and each of the guys held a can of beer in one hand—including the driver. Out of the frying pan, into the fire, I couldn't help thinking. I hoped all of Mr. Walker's blessings were enough to carry me to the end of this ride.

"Hey, man, want a beer?" asked purple pants.

I thought for a second. I didn't really want a beer, but something told me that to not accept would appear un-friendly. "Sure. Thanks."

"Where ya headed?" asked the first guy who had spo-ken. "My name's Jeff, by the way."

"Bud." I shook his hand. This time I took my name from the beer can, and then I realized how ridiculous that was. "Uh, real name's Walter, but everyone calls me Bud."

"Hey. This Bud's for you," joked purple pants.

I tried to smile like I'd heard that joke at least twelve thousand times before. "I'm headed for Detroit." Maybe these guys were going there, too. I snapped open the can of beer and looked at it. I had had beer before, of course. I hadn't liked it much but I knew I couldn't show that to these guys—they'd probably take it as a personal insult. I decided I'd mostly pretend to drink it and just take it really slowly. In Texas—probably everywhere—most guys my age had gotten drunk a few times at least, but I never had. It wasn't that I was a wimp—well, not totally. I just could picture what would hit the fan if my dad ever caught me. He didn't drink at all, but it wasn't even that—it would have been the underage part of it. My dad has this real law-abiding way about him—well, now, of course I knew why. I guess I learned my "don't-get-noticed" ways from him. I took a sip of the beer and was surprised to find that it tasted good. Sweetish, but not all sweet like pop. Very refreshing. I took another swig. Well, I guess it was like they said, it's an acquired taste, and, somehow, I had acquired it. I took another swig. Boy, it tasted good.

"Bud? Hey, Bud?" Jeff was saying.

"Hm? Oh, sorry, man. Musta zoned out. Tired. What did you say?"

"We're heading north, not going to Detroit, but we can take you to Ann Arbor. You can probably get there from there."

Ann Arbor! That was way the other side of Toledo. I might make it over the border in time after all.

"What's in Detroit?" asked the driver.

"Work. My brother got me a job there."

"Work? In Detroit?" The driver seemed amazed.

"Actually, it's more *near* Detroit than *in*," I corrected myself, hoping I was convincing.

"What kind of work?" asked purple pants.

"Oh, man, don't talk about work!" said the dark-haired guy, who had been silent up to now. "We're on VA-CA-*TION*!"

The other three chimed in with yells and yahoos. Purple pants tried out a little air guitar.

I grinned and took another gulp of beer. It was the last gulp in the can.

"Aren't you a little young? I mean, to be out of school, working ...?" the driver trailed off.

I tried to look bored. "I get that all the time. It's such a hassle. And the only chicks you can get are like—" I cut myself off and made a face.

"'Nother beer?" asked purple pants, tossing it to me without waiting for an answer. "We've got lots."

It wasn't a very good idea. Somewhere inside, I knew it wasn't a very good idea, but I couldn't locate the exact place in my head where I had that piece of information. I snapped open the can.

The next part of the ride was a blur of "Road trip!" and high fives, air guitars and smoke. Not even an hour had gone by in the van when I began to feel strange. It was probably that smoke, maybe the beer, maybe not enough to eat, maybe the tension. But the cause didn't matter as much as the effect. I was going to puke.

If I told these guys, would they stop and let me puke, and then let me get back in the car? Not likely. If I puked out the window, they'd probably kick me out, too. But I needed the ride through Toledo. Was there any way I could keep it down? I swallowed hard. I could feel that rolling feeling in my stomach. It would feel good to chuck up the beer and get on with it, but I couldn't lose this ride. I swallowed again and burped slightly, carefully, to see if I could get rid of the nausea feeling. I could taste the beer and that sour taste that comes with puke. I swallowed, again.

"Hey, man!" purple pants yelled suddenly. "The kid's gonna hurl! Pull over!" So much for the ride to Toledo.

The van swerved to the side of the road and the guy called Jeff flung the door open. I staggered out and Jeff threw my pack out after me. Even before the door was closed again, the van was halfway back onto the road. Goodbye to the ride past Toledo. I turned my back on the road and puked my guts inside out.

At first it felt good to have the rolling feeling gone from my stomach, but when I finished throwing up the beer, the chocolate bar, and the hash browns, there was nothing but disgusting sour bile coming up. I finally stopped heaving and made my way to a picnic table that wasn't far from the road. I was at some kind of a rest stop—it seemed to be the entrance to a state park. I realized I had to stop and do some thinking, which was kind of hard since I was still a little drunk, or a bit loopy, anyway.

First, though, food. I sat on the top of the picnic table. All I had was four more of those chocolate bars I bought from Paula a lifetime ago and the apple Reverend Walker had given me. I just couldn't face chocolate, though, so the apple it was—even if it *was* poisoned. I polished it hard on my sleeve to get it as clean as I could, and bit in. It was sweet and juicy, and so tasting of home that I almost cried. What was I doing here? What was Chris Ramsay, fifteen-year-old regular kid from just outside Dallas, doing in a rest stop in Ohio on a Sunday afternoon, making a break for the Canadian border, lying my way across America, living on chocolate and other people's beer and apples, lank-haired, dirty, haggard, lost and lonely, not far from a pool of my own vomit? Maybe I should forget about this ridiculous quest. Maybe I should just go home.

Just then, I heard a car turn into the rest stop area. Looking up, I saw it was a cop car. It was simple, then. All I had to do was turn myself in and I'd be home and warm and clean in no time. But home where? I couldn't just go back and pretend everything was the same as before. No, I'd started something and I felt kind of like the cars on a roller-coaster. You're in, and they get hooked onto that belt thing that pulls them up the first hill. The ride is on and there's no going back.

I tensed a little as the cop car crawled nearer and the window rolled down.

"Everything all right here?" called the cop.

I swallowed, then faked a cheery smile (I hoped) and waved my half-eaten apple. I pointed to my backpack. "Hiking. Just waiting for my pickup." Was there even a hiking trail in this park? I hoped like hell there was.

"How far did you walk?"

"Not that far—five miles or so." I indicated my shabby appearance. "Got a little off the trail to check out some animal tracks, so I'm not sure exactly."

"Are you from around here, son?"

"Oh. No." How long could I keep this up? "Visiting my cousin. The one that's coming to pick me up. He went back for the car 'cause I got a bit of a blister. He should be here in a little while."

I guess I hit the right notes because the cops seemed satisfied.

"We'll check back in a bit and see you got your ride okay. Take care." The window rolled up and the car crept on out of the rest area. Still, I didn't quite relax until they were out of sight.

But now what to do? I had to get going before the cops came back and I really couldn't walk on the road, since they might spot me. I was still over an hour by car from Canada, and I hadn't noticed many cars on this road. And it was getting late and a little overcast. I shivered as I realized that my dad might already be starting to wonder why I hadn't come back from camping with Brian. I thought about finding a hiding spot and spending the night out here at the rest stop but, no, it was way too urgent to get over the border before he realized I was gone. Besides, if it rained ... I tossed the apple core into the nearby wire basket as another car pulled into the rest stop. The back doors burst open and three little girls ran for the outhouses at the back of the parking area. More slowly, the front doors of the old green Volvo opened, and the parents, or whoever they were, of the little girls got out of the car, stretching and sighing.

The parents were dressed like hippies, a bit. The dad had

a short beard and he was wearing one of those cotton pull-overs with a hood. The mom's hair was long and blondy-gray, tied in a braid, and she was wearing a long skirt and a thick beige sweater with patterns knitted in it in brown. Both had on Birkenstock sandals, and the car bumper had stickers on it: *Nuclear-free car; Hug a dolphin today.* It was almost a joke, really; it was too classic. But then I noticed something that was no joke at all. Ontario license plates. Ontario. If I could get into that car, I might make it over the border after all. But how to do it?

The first little girl, the one with the kinky black hair, was running back from the outhouse, yelling about how stinky it was. Would the family (if they were, because they were kind of a United Nations of kids) stay, maybe have a picnic or something? Or would they just travel on as soon as all the girls were back? *Think fast, think fast.* Somehow, I had to get their attention, strike up a conversation, get them to offer me a ride. *Come on, Chris, think.*

But all my brain would do as I watched the second little girl return was spin. I felt that sick, rolling feeling again but, this time, it seemed different. I sure didn't want to puke in front of them; there'd be no way they'd offer me a ride then. I stood up, and as I stood, I realized what was wrong with me. My legs turned to jelly, I was going to ...

Black out.

I was only unconscious on the ground for a second or two, I thought, and now I was realizing that I was going to have to make the effort to get up. But when I opened my eyes, the mom from the Volvo was already kneeling next to me, with the dad's face hovering higher up.

"Are you all right?" the mom was saying.

Obviously not, I thought, but I tried to nod. Don't blow this chance. In a moment, I was able to sit up.

"What happened?" asked the mom. I looked at her un-made-up face, her concerned blue eyes, her messy hair, and I just wanted to trust her, wanted to throw myself into her arms and cry and tell her the truth. But trusting people was what got me here. I couldn't, not so close to my goal. No weakness now. My head felt like sore fog.

"I don't know," I replied. "I haven't had much to eat." That was true. You could take inventory about eight feet away.

"Claire, run and get some trail mix from the car," the mom told the oldest girl, who looked about ten. She didn't seem to want to leave this most fascinating exhibit, but she went and was back in no time.

I used munching on the trail mix as a stall to gather my thoughts. At least I was on speaking terms with these peo-ple now, but were they going to want a dirty, starving teen-ager in their car? What would I tell them?

"Are you running away?" asked Claire, who had been staring at me all the time I ate. I nearly choked on a sun-flower seed. And then I realized ... this could work. This time, I might actually admit that part of the truth.

"Yes."

"Your mother must be worried about you," said the mom.

As seen on TV, I thought. "I doubt it," I snorted. "They

want to get rid of me anyhow. They were planning to send me away—I'm just makin' it easy for 'em."

"What do you mean?"

Here I go again, lying, I thought. But I had to; it was my only chance. I looked over at the dad. If these people still looked like hippies this far on, I figured, then they'd probably held onto some of their ideals, too. "They want to send me to *military* school. Fat chance!"

I watched the parents exchange glances. "Why?" asked the mom.

"They say I'm a handful. I'm too much to handle. Just 'cause they caught me smoking a joint." I hate to admit it, but I've never even seen such a thing. I only hoped that I had the terminology right. Probably. I saw that on TV, too.

"Where are you going?"

"Well, that's the trouble. I have an uncle who lives in Canada. I want to go to his place, but I don't know if they'll let me over the border. I lost my ID."

"How?"

"I was sleeping in a bus station and I got robbed. Pretty stupid. That's why I haven't been eating much."

"But won't your uncle just send you back to your parents?" chimed in Claire. She was a smart one, that one.

I turned on my most charming smile. I was pretty sure this was the kicker. "Nah. He was a draft dodger—Viet Nam. He'll let me stay."

Again, the parents exchanged a glance. "What's his name? We might know him."

Yikes. Why would they know him? "Um ... Uncle Jeff.

Jeff, uh, Van ... Van Stone." I just made it up from fragments from my last ride and the uncomfortable lump under my left leg.

The parents shook their heads. "Can you excuse us for a second ... um ..."

"Brian," I said, trying to act friendly. I was so tired, I could only think of my old best friend's name. (Old best friend? It was only yesterday morning I woke up in my "old" best friend's room. It was ten lives ago.)

"Hi, Brian, I'm Andrea, this is Steve. The girls are Claire, Meghan, and Heather." I smiled at them each in turn— blond, dark hair with braids, frizzy black. "Look, I was just going to offer you a ride, at least to Windsor. Okay with you, Steve?"

Steve hesitated. "Do you think it's a good idea? It *would* be illegal."

"Illegal!" Andrea laughed. "We were practically running the Underground Railroad for draft dodgers twenty-five years ago. What's one more?" I watched them carefully. This was better than I could have hoped. Would it work?

Steve looked at the girls with some concern. "All right," he sighed and shook his head.

Yes!

Tucked in the back seat with Claire and Meghan, and pretty little Heather sitting up front, I felt better than I had so far on this trip. Andrea kept feeding me trail mix, fruit, cheese, and crackers. Claire bombarded me with questions, and I was sorry to notice that I had become a very smooth liar in the last two days: Where was I from? (Galveston, I said.) What grade was I in? (Eleventh, I said.) How old was I? (Sixteen, I said.) Did I have a girlfriend? (Paula, I said.) What was I good at? (Baseball, I said.) Where did my Uncle live? (Toronto, I said.) Was it on my mother's side or my father's side? (Mother's, I said.) Had I ever been to Canada before? (No, I said. Even that was a lie. I was born in Canada. Did it matter? Had I completely forgotten the difference between lies and truth?)

The car pulled onto the freeway system around Toledo and Meghan curled up beside me and fell asleep. The car smelled of home. Not my home, but some imaginary home from the movies and commercials that came on TV at Christmas time, and the sappier sitcoms. It wasn't a specific smell, just the mingling smells of clean hair and things to eat and comfort. This was what home was supposed to be like. A place where the mom put her hand on the back of the dad's neck and exchanged a smile with him, filled with meaning that they both understood, filled with the time they had shared together. A place where things were allowed to be messy. Claire played a soft little tune on a harmonica she had pulled out of her *OshKosh B'Gosh* overalls pocket (that's what it said on the pocket). Before long, I had been lulled to sleep, too, as the Volvo sped up the I-75 to Detroit, and the border, and a new country I didn't know.

My stomach growled a little and woke me up. The trail mix had been great but I would have liked an actual meal. I kept my eyes closed as I pictured a juicy hamburger, with cheese maybe.

"Brian," came Andrea's voice, gently, and I opened my eyes.

"Mmmh?" I stretched my arms a little, not wanting to wake up Meghan.

"You might have to lie to get over the border. Are you okay with that?"

I almost laughed out loud when she said that, but I kept my wits and nodded soberly, as if it was something I didn't want to do but had to.

"Pretend you're asleep as we cross the border. But if they make you wake up, we'll agree that you're our son, then?" I nodded again. "And you don't have ID on you. Since we're returning home, they shouldn't be as particular as if we were going the other way."

"Okay." Now that I thought about it, I actually really didn't like the idea of lying to the customs guy. Everyone else I'd lied to was just people, but this would be actually illegal.

"Okay, so where were you born?" Andrea grilled me.

"Canada."

"You sound like that President Bush!" squealed Claire. "Kyanada!"

"Say it," I prompted her.

"Canada." It sounded like "Cahn-ada" to me.

"Cahn-ada."

"Not Connada!"

I tried again. "Cah-nada."

"No, not Cawnada. Try again. Canada."

"Caa-nada."

"Try not to talk." Claire folded her arms across her chest.

"Play the harmonica some more," I urged Claire, and she did. She showed me how it worked, getting different notes, and I even learned "Old Macdonald." Sort of. Well, everyone pretended I did. Probably so I'd stop trying.

Steve shifted in the driver's seat, sitting up straighter. "Border's soon."

Andrea smiled at me encouragingly. "Better look asleep."

Feeling more nervous than ever, I closed my eyes and tried to get comfortable. Please, Mr. Customs Guy, don't wake me up.

Soon the Volvo began to slow and I opened my eyes just a crack to see that we had joined a line of cars crossing a bridge.

This was it, then. The Canadian border.

I closed my eyes again.

The car moved forward, with me inside, car length by car length, one at a time.

I pictured the little car on my Formica world map, inching closer to Canada.

As the car pulled up at the Customs and Immigration booth, I found it was almost impossible to keep my eyes shut. I was here. The international border. My stomach churned, my chest felt tight, tingles ran down my arms. The moment I had raced across half of America for, the moment I had most dreaded, the moment I would most likely be caught—had my dad called the police yet?—was going to pass as a moment I would not see. Would the customs guy peer at me suspiciously? Would he be friendly? Would he let us go, or stop and search these hippie freaks? Had I taken the very worst ride I could have chosen, if I could have chosen anything? The brakes squeaked lightly as the car pulled up, fresh air tinged with carbon monoxide and diesel exhaust wafting in as Steve rolled the window down.

"Citizens of what country?" came a man's voice.

"Canada," said Steve.

"Canada," said Andrea.

"How long have you been in the U.S.?"

"Since Friday," said Steve.

"Purpose of your visit?"

"Visiting friends," said Steve.

"What are you bringing back?"

Me. I tried to look asleep, relaxed, unmoving, so as not to draw attention to myself, yet not stiff, so as not to seem fake. Yes, relaxed, as my entire fate rested in this moment. It was just about impossible.

"Nothing," said Steve.

For a moment, nothing was said. What was happening? Why had they stopped talking, yet the car hadn't moved forward? Meghan stirred and dug her elbow sharply into my ribs. Against all the laws of physics and human nature, I stayed still. What was going on?

"Is this your dad?" the customs guy asked Claire.

"Yes, he is."

"What about the boy? Can you wake him up, please?"

Oh, no.

"Where were you born?"

Oh, no.

"Cah-nada," I hoped I said. It was actually true! But I couldn't let anything show.

The customs officer looked at me a moment, then nodded.

"Okay." The car started away. I breathed normally again for the first time in two or three centuries. And, of course, I couldn't let anything show to this family, either. I hoped they would take my relief at not having to lie to the customs guy as just general relief at having made it. I really hadn't lied. I hadn't broken the law.

"See?" Andrea said, grinning at Steve. "Piece of cake." Steve just tipped his head. Obviously, taking runaways over international borders wasn't his favorite flavor of cake.

"It's done," was all he said.

"Did I say it right?" I asked Claire. She tipped her hand like a seesaw to say, "more or less."

Andrea was almost giggly. "Well, Brian ... do you feel like a fugitive? Like a refugee?"

I wasn't sure how I felt. Relieved, for sure. But now, also, strangely scared. Somewhere in the back of my mind, I suppose I'd never truly believed I'd make it this far. I'd crossed into a foreign country. I guess I really thought I'd be caught and turned back. What I would have done then, I don't know. I had made the break, but now I wasn't even sure why. Was life so bad with my dad? Brian had

been right: I *was* out of my mind to be doing this!

I grinned at Andrea and tried not to look as worried as I felt. "Weird," was all I said, and then remembered their version of my story. "I've escaped military school." And then I thought about the rigid way my father had always run the household and realized: I was almost telling the truth, sort of. Maybe not literally military school, but I was leaving behind the dinner schedules, the army-corner beds, routines, routines, routines, and disapproval. Ramsay Men, according to my dad.

So now I was over the border, with a disturbing thought in my head. I had always, I guess, kind of half thought it wasn't real, that I could always turn back, that I *would* turn back, but I couldn't, not now. I'd never get back across the border unnoticed, and it was too late now, anyway. In fact, my father was probably right this minute figuring out that I was gone. But I was scared to go forward or, at least, all the way forward.

"You can stay the night with us, if you like," said Andrea, as if she could read my mind. "You can call your uncle and tell him you're safe and on your way. We live just outside Windsor. It's not too far away."

What—really? I could stay with them? "No, no thanks," I said, shaking my head, though I longed to say yes. What I wanted to say was, can't I live with you? Can't I just stay? Can't I have a nice mom and dad and three cute little sisters? But I couldn't *not* call my supposed uncle, and I didn't have anyone *to* call—I didn't even know what the area code for Toronto might be. And even though I was

over the border, I wanted to leave it far behind me, in case the customs people could catch up to me and pull me back. They probably could, actually. There would probably still be border patrols ahead, like there are in southern Texas, to catch Mexicans even after they get over the border. I hadn't even thought about that before. I'd better get far away.

I tried to decide what to do next. I only had eighty-five dollars left, and I knew a bus would eat up a lot of it. But I just couldn't face any more uncertainty, at least for a while. "Could you put me somewhere I can get a bus to the bus station?"

"We can take you to the station," said Andrea. "Are you sure you won't stay?"

"No, I think I'd just like to get to Uncle Jeff's. Thanks for everything, though. I mean it."

As the Volvo pulled up in front of the bus station, Claire, who had run out of conversation just before Detroit, suddenly piped up. "How are you going to get a bus ticket?"

What did she mean? How could she have known I'd been getting other people to buy them for me? "Huh?"

"I thought you got your wallet stolen," she replied.

Oh, yeah.

"Well, I ..." I thought furiously. "Actually, I have some money in my pack. I didn't put it all in my wallet. Luckily."

Claire looked at me like she could see what I had in my pack, my pocket, like she could see my bones and the little suitcase key in my stomach that I had swallowed when I was six. I had the feeling she knew

I was lying this time, but I wasn't sure what to do.

"We'd better wait and make sure there's another bus tonight," said Andrea.

Steve turned off the engine and everyone piled out of the car. I went to the trunk to retrieve my pack. When Steve had the trunk lid open and we were screened from view of the others, he suddenly turned to me.

"Here, kid," he said, pressing a bit of purple-and-ivory-colored paper into my hand. "It could come in handy."

I looked. It looked like money. Funny-looking, funny-colored money.

"I couldn't," I said. But I could, I really could. "You guys have done enough."

Just then, Andrea came into sight.

"Forget it," muttered Steve, and made his hands busy so I couldn't give it back. I slipped the bill into my back pocket.

"Thanks again."

"Let's go in and check on the bus," said Andrea.

"I'll stay with the car. We don't want to get towed. Good luck, Brian." Steve shook my hand.

"Bye," I said, feeling sort of awful now that he'd done so much for me and I hadn't even told him my right name.

As the girls and Andrea went ahead of me, I managed to fumble my money out of my wallet and into my front pocket so Claire wouldn't catch me out.

The ticket cost almost fifty dollars in Canadian money. They took thirty-five American bucks off me. That left me fifty for food and to get to Kingston, which looked on the map to be almost as far away from Toronto as Windsor was.

Oh, well. I'd figure out what to do when I got to Toronto.

"Look," said Andrea, as I put the rest of my money back in my pocket. "You might need this." She was shoving some greenish paper into my hand. It was money again— this time with a big "twenty" written on it. Weird, how they had different colors for their money here.

"No, you guys have done enough for me. Really."

"Just take it, silly," insisted Andrea. "You'll need some Canadian cash to get around. Go. They're calling your bus."

"Bye. It's been really nice meeting you guys. You saved my life, you really did." They really did.

Claire hadn't said anything since the comment about the wallet and was still giving me a suspicious look. Now she spoke. "I like you," she said. And suddenly, she shoved the harmonica into my jacket pocket.

I felt stabbed through the heart. I almost wanted to cry. *I want to stay! I want to stay! Why can't you be my little sister?*

"No." I fished out the harmonica and pointed it back at her. She folded her arms across her chest and looked mad. I glanced at Andrea, who just tilted her head slightly.

Back to Claire. "I like you, too." And I turned away fast and went for the bus, slipping the harmonica into my pocket, the cool metal sides between my fingers.

A few minutes later, in the bus as it rounded the front of the station, I could see them all by the car, Steve on the driver's side behind the open door, Heather in Andrea's arms, waving, Claire waving, and Meghan just watching me, with a thumb in her mouth. I put my hand up to the window and watched them out of sight, then closed my hand to hold the memory, like taking a picture, like I had the last time I'd seen Paula, painting her toenails on the front porch. I was so exhausted, so relieved, so sad, so scared, I closed my eyes to keep from just crying.

The scenery on the way to Toronto was nothing special. Flat, open fields for a while, like home. Then, just highway, lined with small manufacturers and other companies. No seatmates this time, so I was glad, though it would have been all right if it were someone like Beatrice. I wondered if she was having fun with her dad. And then that made me think about my dad. Did I ever have fun with him? Fun wasn't really a word I associated with him. He was probably a good kid-raiser. He always made his expectations clear. He wasn't stingy, although we weren't too rich. But like with Rover—he didn't play with him. He wasn't too upset when he ran away—in fact, he got rid of his bowls and leash and stuff pretty quickly, like he already knew Rover wasn't coming back.

The ride was uneventful and I dozed a little. The bus stopped at two places, London and Kitchen-something (weird). They both seemed like pretty large cities. No border patrols or, at least, none that stopped us, though I was tense throughout the ride, just waiting to be caught. It was starting to get dark and it was still cloudy, but the rain had held off so far, or else I'd dodged it.

It was completely dark by the time we pulled in sight of Toronto. I could see the whole city across part of the lake. Boy, that lake seemed huge. I couldn't even see any shore or lights on the other side. I knew the Great Lakes were big, I'd looked at them often enough on my desk map, but I'd never realized that this one, which was one of the small ones, was so big you couldn't see across it. Suddenly thinking of my desk like that gave me a really weird feeling. Instead of picturing me in a minibus driving across it, I actually wondered if I would ever see that desk again. I had spent more time there, dreaming about the places I might visit than doing my homework. And now, and now, here I was. On it.

The city was beautiful, a glittering place that looked like you'd need money in it. It was big, as big as Dallas, it looked like, with skyscrapers in the center, and a pointed tower that I had seen on TV when the Rangers played the Blue Jays. And there *was* the Skydome, with its roof that could slide open and where Tom Henke, my favorite non-Ranger, closed games with dizzying coolness. He had actually started his Major League career as a Ranger, but that was when I was a baby. The bus climbed down from an elevated highway, sailed up a broad avenue and pulled into its bay in the bus terminal. I glanced at my watch. Ten forty-five at night. Now what?

When I stepped down into the cavernous bus station, I didn't see that there was much point in going inside the waiting room area. I couldn't exactly spend the night there without being seen, and it was probably best if nobody noticed me arrive in town. Tomorrow, I could find out about buses to Kingston. Tonight, I just had to stop moving. But first, I had to find a place to stop.

I left the bus station and, having no idea where I was or even which direction I was facing any more, I arbitrarily turned right. I soon came to what was obviously the grandest street in the city, wide, with boulevards in the middle, and big statues, and boring-type office buildings lining the road. Right now, it was dark and there wasn't that much traffic. I had no idea where I was going.

Probably there were teen shelters and stuff in Toronto, if I knew where they were. But I wasn't sixteen yet, so probably they'd be filled with do-gooders who'd send me back home or, actually, turn me over to the cops. I just kept hoping I'd come to a park or something where I could sleep. One with a bandstand or some kind of shelter, because

I still wasn't sure it wasn't going to rain. I figured there might be something like that by the lake, though I hadn't really noticed anything on my way into town, but that was the direction I headed in, anyway, downhill, back toward the lake. As I waited at the stoplight, an enormous red and white trolley car rolled by and clanged its bell, which was pretty cool. After that, I noticed the tracks built into a couple more of the streets I was crossing.

The buildings were very big, like downtown Dallas, and I felt quite small walking among them. I could see that tower every now and then. It was really tall. Although I knew I was going toward the lake, it was much farther than it seemed like it should be.

The road curved down and into a tunnel. A tedious walk through the tunnel took me out to walk another block, and then the route took me under the highway I realized must be the one I had come into town on. After that, I came out to a big old boat terminal or something and just high-rises, some open spaces, and a few boats that could be rented or you could pay for a ride on. There were trolley cars around there, too, but they had their own part of the road. I walked along the water's edge, but I didn't see anything that looked like it would work. Anyway, there were people strolling around, so I'd probably get told to move on. It was really dark, so I turned up the first major-looking street I came to. I was nearly stumbling with exhaustion when I felt the first large raindrop plant a sloppy kiss on my face. A few more droplets hit the pavement around me and, suddenly, it was really raining. I darted for the shelter of the elevated highway up ahead to wait for the rain to blow over.

But it didn't, and I felt myself starting to fall asleep standing up, so, finally, I pulled my sleeping bag out of my pack and made myself a little bed between two pillars.

Tired as I was, it was hard to go to sleep on the concrete ground. I kept waiting to be arrested. Or mugged. I wasn't sure which I would prefer.

Daylight woke me, and the only reason I knew I'd slept at all was the sense that I'd had a dream, but I couldn't remember it. Well, Beatrice, at least I wouldn't go crazy. It had been bitterly cold all night and, though I was dying to sleep, it was just too uncomfortable and scary, sleeping under a city bridge, to be restful. I woke up hungry and feeling dirtier than I'd ever felt, even camping, and I knew my eyes were red—I could feel them—and I was pretty sure my deodorant had expired, and as I rubbed my face to try to wake up, I felt real stubble—well, that was kind of interesting—and I really, really had to take a whiz.

This I managed behind a pillar—there wasn't all that much traffic around yet, since it was pretty early, but I figured my best bet was heading back to the bus station, where I could probably wash my face and maybe get something to eat and figure out what to do next. I rolled up my sleeping bag and packed it away and began trudging up the street.

Traffic was getting a lot busier, and I realized it was actually Monday and it must be rush hour. On my right was the white Skydome stadium—huge and beautiful. Its roof was closed. Dome today, no sky. I recognized some of the street names from last night, so I knew I was going the right way.

As I trekked uphill toward the bus station, I scarfed down another chocolate bar. I hadn't had a real meal since Saturday and I could have eaten my sleeping bag, but I didn't want to spend anything until I knew what the bus ticket would cost, and I thought I'd better not eat the sleeping bag till I was sure I didn't need it anymore.

The street was more interesting than yesterday's—there were coffee shops and clothes stores and, slowly, it turned into Chinatown. All the signs were bright red and yellow, sometimes green. There was all kinds of merchandise, in bins outside the stores, labeled with prices in English and Chinese, from baskets and sandals to fruits and vegetables I'd never seen before, and unusual kinds of greens that I wondered whether my father would count as "something green" with dinner.

That made me think about home and I wondered what was happening there. My father must have called Brian's by now, and I wondered how he would react once he realized I hadn't been camping and must have taken off. Until a week ago, I would have known exactly what he would do, but a week ago, I lived in a different reality. The thought made me dizzy and a little sick. I kind of wanted to cry. Grab hold. Think about it later.

Standing waiting for a traffic light to change to green, I gradually realized there were a couple of kids not much older than me, darting among the traffic. They were washing windshields, apparently for tips. I had heard of homeless men doing that kind of thing in Dallas, but I'd never seen kids—or anyone, really—at it. The boy was tall and skinny, with matted, long dark hair and a small beard, and the girl was small, might have been pretty, except she was just plain weird-looking. I watched her through a whole light change, with her black boots and head shaved on one side—long black hair from one side, red brush cut from the other. And I don't mean Nicole Kidman red; I mean red-red. The red side's ear had at least seven earrings, and the black side had an eyebrow ring with a chain leading to a nose ring. Heavy black eyeliner and lipstick—black lipstick!—meant that you couldn't really see what she looked like, just the skin she had created for herself. She looked like something out of New York City. Maybe there were girls like that in downtown Dallas, but I had never seen one. Not that I went there much.

The lights changed again and the windshields moved on. The two kids weaved back through the moving traffic toward the sidewalk. I couldn't stop looking at the girl. She had on a really short kilt—a school uniform?—and a white T-shirt. I really tried not to, but I couldn't help noticing that she wasn't wearing a bra. I like to think of myself as brought up to be, well, a gentleman (by that snake?), so I dragged my eyes away, in time to catch a yellow streak on a bicycle that was bearing down on her, somehow not seeing her, somehow not veering, somehow not stopping.

It was like slow motion and fast motion and stop motion

all at once, but I had to do *something*. "Hey!" I shouted. Nothing changed, the bike was nearly on her. I leaped forward, grabbed her arm, pulled her toward the sidewalk, tangling my feet with hers, knocking us both down.

"Fucking squeegee kids!" the cyclist yelled as he rode on, not even caring whether the girl was all right.

"Fuck you, fucker!" the girl yelled back, sitting up and giving the cyclist the finger. Apparently, she was all right. "Not you," she turned to me, speaking in a normal voice. "I'm Moth. You saved my life, I guess. Fucking bike couriers. I'll give you three wishes. What'll it be?" Or maybe she wasn't all right. Maybe she'd hit her head or something. Maybe it was my fault for knocking her over.

"Are you okay?" I asked her. I wasn't sure *I* was. "I mean ... are you okay? Are you hurt? I'm Chris." We were sitting side by side on the pavement. I thought we might have gathered a crowd but, when I glanced up, the only one paying attention to us was the dark-haired skinny guy.

"Yeah, I'm fine," said Moth.

"Come on," said the guy. "The light's changed."

"Hey, Pilot, you can't go out and do windows when somebody's just saved your life. Come on, this is Chris. I have to grant his three wishes." By this time, we were all standing, and Moth was brushing off a dusty mark on the palm of her fingerless gloves. "Chris—Pilot." She looked up at me and I turned into water inside. Moth was beautiful, in spite of all the junk she had on her face. She was tiny and her eyes were pure green, her face pale-skinned and oval. Her black-painted mouth was a little bit pouty but just this side of spoiled, and her smile was like turning on a light. But I kept coming back to her eyes. They weren't just green, they had gold flecks of sunlight and innocence, they had dark shadows of knowledge and pain. They were eyes that held you, and knew who you were, and didn't judge you. They were eyes that understood and seemed to say, "It's all right," before you even realized anything was wrong. And right now, they were asking me a question. They seemed to ask me where I came from, and who I was, and why I was standing here, though her voice only asked, "What do you want? I'm serious about the three wishes."

"I ... I don't know." I looked at Pilot, who said nothing, only looked back at me.

"Tell you what," said Moth. "Sit here—" she waved her squeegee at a concrete tree planter "—and while you think, we'll do some more windows. Then we'll go get breakfast."

I did as I was told and sat on the tree planter, hugging my pack on my lap. Even though Moth had been the one nearly run down, I felt like *I* was the victim of a collision. I watched as Pilot and Moth darted among the cars, hoisted their squeegees, flashed a smile, quickly washed the windshields, and took their tips. I noticed they never washed the windshields when the people quickly shook their heads, but if the drivers weren't quick, it was too late. Some people stared ahead, stony faced, and refused to tip, even when they had clean windshields, and Pilot and Moth gave those ones rude gestures as they drove away, but mostly they were friendly and energetic, and most people seemed pretty okay about the whole thing, a few a little scared. I could imagine feeling scared if a girl like that looked in my car window, but then I remembered her magical eyes and I knew what her secret weapon was. Even though her black eyeliner hid her real face, it also drew you to her eyes, and I knew that she was just mesmerizing the drivers into submission.

After a while, the traffic died down a little, and Pilot emptied the water bucket into the gutter. The two of them tossed their squeegees into the bucket, along with a bottle of glass cleaner. I guess they mixed it with water for the windshields. Moth threw an embroidered bag that I hadn't noticed before over her head and across her body.

"Come on." Moth grabbed my hand—my hand!—as I swung my pack onto my back. "Let's eat. I want to know all about you, Sir Chris, my gallant knight. We have to get you a better name, though."

It was only then that I realized that this was the first time since Friday that I'd given my real name.

There was a McDonald's just a couple of blocks down from where I had been sitting, and that's where we went for breakfast. The guy behind the counter was kind of older, and I thought he might give us a funny look, or maybe kick us out, since those two were pretty wild looking, and I didn't like to think how bad I must look, but he didn't seem to notice or care. Of course, Moth and Pilot probably came here all the time.

I ordered a coffee and an Egg McMuffin (cheap), but when I went to pay for it, Moth waved me away.

"Come on, we're working stiffs. You're probably broke—or will be soon."

I was grateful and, anyway, I couldn't have said no to her whatever she asked me. We took a table by the window. The scene was really lively, with six lanes of traffic, cars, trucks and buses, and people walking, driving, and cycling *everywhere*. Every kind of people, all in a hurry.

"Now, Chris." Moth had my full attention again. "Tell us about yourself."

I paused to think what I would tell her, but she stopped

me before I could speak. "No, wait, let me."

Moth took my hand, unrolled my fingers, and gazed at my palm. "Let's see ... you're running away from home ... because you hate your father. Your mother is ... not strong ... not there? Anyway, not able to get between you. You've come a fairly long way—from the States, I think—and ... you thought you had a plan, but now you're not so sure." She closed my hand and pushed it away. "Well? Am I right?"

I felt dizzy. I hadn't said more than a few words to her. How could she possibly know all this about me? I searched her face for a clue and saw her eyes again. I felt like she was trying to speak to me in some code that I couldn't quite crack, sending a psychic message or something. I grasped around for words.

"Yes, but how did you know?"

"Easy," said Pilot. "It's practically everyone's story around here."

"Except for the American part," said Moth. "That I got from your accent. Where are you from? Texas?"

"Yeah." I suddenly felt like I was drawling. I don't think Texans drawl—I just think everybody else speaks way too fast. But I know outsiders think Texans drawl.

"Now, we need to get you a better name," said Moth. "And a plan. And your three wishes. The plan can be one of them. Tell us your story. Really."

"You pretty much got it. I left Saturday, told my dad I was going camping with a friend. He'll know I'm missing by now."

"Why? What made you leave?"

I knew why I left that particular day, at that particular moment. But I had gotten so used to lying about why I was on the road, to avoid getting caught, hauled back, that I just shrugged. Anyway, to tell it would sound ridiculous. And I'd learned that people would rather talk about themselves anyway, and you could usually deflect a question with a question.

"What's *your* story?" I asked.

"The usual. 'Continental' stepdaddy. You know, Roman hands and Russian fingers." Moth wiggled her fingers to show that she meant "roamin'" and "rushin'". "Tell you the truth, I think my mom was probably glad to see me go—didn't like the competition. So I flew away from North Bay to the big city lights—that's why I named myself Moth."

"What about you, Pilot? Did you run away, too?"

"Yeah."

"Why?"

"Didn't like it at home."

"Where's home?" Might as well be polite, even though I'd never heard of Moth's North Bay, and probably wouldn't know the place Pilot came from.

"Out west. Saskatch'wan."

"Saskatoon?" I had always thought that was one of the best names in the world. Saskatoon, Saskatchewan. It was on my desk map.

"Near there."

"Is your name really Pilot?"

"No. Gilbert," he answered, making a face.

"Why are you called Pilot?"

"He'd like to fly," said Moth. "Funny, isn't it, we're both called after flying things? And now we're friends. Maybe we should give you a flying name, too. What made you come *here*, though? Why Toronto?" She said it "Tronno."

"Well, I'm not staying here, really. I'm looking for my—" No, wait. What if there was a reward out, or something, wouldn't they just turn me in? Nah, there wouldn't be a reward. I wasn't sure if my dad would even call the police. To stall, I began digging around in my backpack.

"I'm looking for my razor, actually, and stuff. I'd better clean up a little or I'll scare the locals." I grabbed my backpack and headed for the men's room.

I locked the door behind me and stood and looked in the mirror, hands on the sides of the sink. I probably might scare the locals, though not as much as Moth and Pilot should. I looked at my new face—and it *was* a new face, with red-rimmed eyes, stringy hair and rough jaw—and asked myself what the hell I was doing.

Moth had basically asked me the same thing. Why *did* I leave? I had convinced myself, convinced Brian (maybe) that I wasn't running away, I was running *to*. But I was beginning to think there was more to it, that maybe I really was running *away*, and I wasn't really going anywhere, didn't really care about solving any mysteries or sorting things out, finding my "mother," whoever she was, that I was just using this all as an excuse to be *gone*.

Here I was, a thousand miles from home, in a foreign country, and all for what? Moth was right: I did need a plan. What was I going to do—go on to Kingston and just start knocking on doors? The realization shook me like a wave. What the hell was I doing?

I sat down on the edge of the toilet and rested my forehead against the cool porcelain of the sink. I had no idea what to do next. My head hurt, my eyes hurt, my back hurt. But my heart didn't hurt. I looked up at my reflection again with the strange understanding that I didn't miss my father. I didn't know who he was to miss. No wonder I couldn't decide how my father would react. I simply didn't know.

And I didn't miss my old self, my old life. I didn't know what that was, either. There was really no point in traveling on to Kingston. I would be going to no place I knew, no place I was needed. It would be a place no more like home than the place I'd left.

In my mind, I even tried to run some scenes from my life, like they do at the end of a movie sometimes. All I could see was the blank bit after the movie was over, or maybe the numbers counting down at the beginning. I didn't really have any pictures in my mind, just like we had no pictures in the house. Except just that one of the kid in the gooberish snowsuit.

Camping, I'd gone with Brian's family. School stuff, my dad was always at work.

So maybe it was time to just make a new home somewhere. Moth and Pilot seemed to have it pretty good—a kind of job, money, good times, it seemed like. Moth said I needed a plan. Maybe she could be part of it.

I shoved the razor back into my pack. What the hell. I looked awful, but so did Moth and Pilot. I might as well fit in.

I came out of the McDonald's washroom, looking the same as when I went in, only with maybe just a tiny bit more of a set to my jaw (I hoped). Moth looked up, smiling.

"Took you long enough. You look the same."

"Yeah," I said, but I didn't feel the same. "I want my first wish—like you said—a plan."

"Come on, then. Let's go to our yacht." Yacht? This made no sense. "You can crash with us for a while." Pilot flashed her a doubtful look. "Come *on!*" Moth pulled Pilot by the arm. "It's not every day we find a fainting robin fallen from its nest. There's plenty of cars later. Come *on!*"

We left the McDonald's, waited as a trolley car rolled past us, and went back down the same street I had walked up just an hour or so earlier. We were passing the stores with all the stuff in bins. Suddenly, Moth grabbed an orange. I couldn't believe how openly she took it, and I was even more shocked when the shop owner shouted and she just laughed and skipped on—didn't even really run. I couldn't help glancing back and seeing the old guy shaking his fist at us. If it had been in a movie, I might even have laughed, but my stomach did a sick twist. This was stealing, from a real person, pure and simple.

"Moth ..." What could I say? I didn't see how I could

teach her right and wrong if she didn't already know it.

"What? Oh, the orange?" Moth let it roll down her arm, bounced the fruit off the inside of her elbow and caught it again. She looked at it and then at me, almost blank. "Hey, we need our vitamins."

I just stood there, feeling helpless and incredibly naïve and young.

"It's only an orange. The guy had hundreds of them."

I still couldn't think of anything to say. I didn't know where to look.

"Boy, what a straight arrow," Moth muttered and shoved the orange into her bag. Her arms were thick with bracelets. She looked mad.

I felt so stupid. I'd caused a problem, yet I hadn't solved the one that bothered me. What good was that? What would Moth and Pilot think of me now? What an idiot I was. These were supposed to be my new friends, my new life, and this was how I started it off?

But it seemed like Moth had already forgotten about it. "Arrow!" she was shouting. "That's a good name for you. 'I shot an arrow in the air. It fell to earth I know not where.'" She grinned sideways at me. I felt a little better. A little.

We soon reached another busy street and crossed the road.

"Come on, there's a streetcar."

The streetcar (good thing I hadn't called it a trolley car) made a clanging sound as it stopped, and Moth scrambled up the steps, followed by Pilot and then me. Moth flounced to the back of the car without paying and sat in the middle of the very back seat. The streetcar moved forward. Pilot dug into his jeans front pocket for money but came up empty.

"Hang on a sec," he said to the streetcar driver and began checking all his pockets. Nowhere did he come up with the money for the fare, but I knew both Pilot and Moth had pocketed quite a few tips when they were cleaning windshields that morning.

"Hey, Zack," yelled Moth from the back of the streetcar. (Zack?) "What'cha doing?"

"Have you got tickets? I don't have them."

"What?" called Moth.

"Tickets."

"What about tickets?"

"Do you have some?"

"No. I thought you had them, you idiot."

"Sorry, man," said Pilot to the streetcar driver.

"Out." said the driver, clanging to a stop again.

"Sure, sorry, no problem," said Pilot politely.

The door folded open and I stepped down first. I had been about to offer to pay their way—after all, they covered breakfast—but when Moth called Pilot "Zack," I knew something was up. Still, it was okay—it wasn't dishonest— we got off and everything. The streetcar rumbled away. Moth was giggling.

"Not bad—three stops. One more streetcar should do it. Let's wait. Hey, Arrow, you're our luck. We've never made it three before! Woo-hoo!"

Oh, great. This was like the bus ride between St. Louis

and Indianapolis. And look what luck stealing that ride brought. I'd lost most of my money right after that. And swore I'd never steal another ride. I didn't want this to be happening.

"Luck's a delicate thing," I said, not looking at either of them. "Can't we walk from here?"

"All right," agreed Moth. "It's not that far now, anyway."

A few more blocks, down a side street and then through a fence, across a field, some railway tracks, and an open concrete area, and I could see the lake sparkling beyond.

"Home, sweet home," announced Moth, indicating a rusted old boat that was pulled up on land and lying on its side. "Welcome to the yacht."

"Well, it's maybe not exactly a yacht," acknowledged Moth. "But it *is* home, sweet home."

Coming from the plains, I don't know much about boats. It wasn't big at all, not a ship, but it looked like it had been some kind of working boat, not a pleasure boat. We crossed the weedy concrete and Moth led the way in, climbing through a front window. I followed, feeling very curious, and found myself standing on the wall of what was once the cockpit, or whatever they call it on boats. The bridge, maybe? Anyway, where the captain would be.

"Our grand foyer," Moth announced.

We ducked and clambered through the sideways doorway into the next area. This looked like it had been a passenger area, though not a very comfortable one. There were bench-type seats jutting out from the floor, which was now the wall, and they were used as shelves. Pots, cloths, and utensils were stashed on them, and in one corner was a folded-up camp stove. I saw the name *Coleman* written on the side of it in red and gold, and it gave me an odd feeling when I saw my mother's maiden name, a splitting feeling. It made me think of camping with Brian, of course, the past, but also, that was the sign on the road ahead, the road I wasn't going to travel. I quickly pushed the feeling aside.

"The banquet hall," Moth was saying.

We climbed through the next door. It was almost pitch dark in this room and, while I waited for my eyes to adjust to the light, I couldn't help noticing the smell. It was a smell like people, but not an honest sweat smell like a locker room, but a thick, heavy smell. Not as strong as smelly feet, just heavy, dirty, like Blake Witter, a boy I knew in grade school, who didn't wash enough. Plus, under it, a faint, dank, mildewy odor. I breathed deeply, just to get enough oxygen, and then I tried not to, to keep the poison-smelling air out of my lungs.

Gradually, my eyes adjusted to the light, and I started to be able to make out light and dark areas against the dark background. They seemed to be piles of rags, but I soon realized they were beds, and there were about six of them. So Moth and Pilot didn't live alone.

"The grand snooze chamber," said Moth finally. "Oh, I know the air isn't too fresh, but you get used to it. It's the warmest part of the boat, and, trust me, you appreciate that when night comes. Anyway, dump your pack—if you like, there's a spot over there—and let's go back to the kitchen. There might be some soup."

I didn't really want to put my pack down in this place. It seemed like there could be lice, or rats, even, and I didn't want to expose my stuff to them. But I didn't want to seem ungrateful, either.

"I don't know ..." I'm not sure where I was going with that but it didn't matter, as it turned out.

"Or bring it. You can sit on it," called Moth, who was rummaging around on the seat-shelves in the next room.

"No soup," she announced, but she didn't seem too concerned. "Now, I think I have your plan. Stay with us; we'll let you share our corner for windshields for a while till you figure it out, then we'll try to find you your own corner, and—stay with us. That's the plan."

I couldn't see anything wrong with the plan. I lifted up an imaginary glass and toasted Moth and Pilot. "To the Plan."

"The Plan."

"The Plan."

So I was going to stay.

"We'd better go back," Pilot said in a moment. "It'll soon be lunch time—we'll miss too many cars if we hang here."

"All right." Moth pouted at him, then she turned to me. "What do you want to do? No point in coming with us till we get you a squeegee. You tired? Want to crash?"

Crash was exactly the right word. A crash landing, here on this rust bucket, to sleep and not wake up for a hundred years.

"Moth ..." said Pilot, but she cut him off.

"He's okay, he's a *baby*. Look at him."

I wasn't sure I liked being classified as a baby, but I supposed that in terms of life on the street, I was. Though

I *had* traveled all the way from Dallas, *and* crossed an international border, which was more than these guys had done. I yawned.

"Go ahead, crash," said Moth. "Keep out of sight and no one will bug you. You'll be safe."

But once they were gone and I had my sleeping bag unrolled in the "grand foyer"—no need to delve into the dank atmosphere of the "grand snooze chamber" in the daytime—I didn't fall asleep. I was tired, but I couldn't really get comfortable. For one thing, what if the other people who lived here came back? What would I say to them? What if they didn't trust me the way Moth did? It seemed like maybe even Pilot didn't trust me completely. And then, when it came to trust, I wasn't sure I trusted Moth—though, somehow I did, too; those green eyes, the way she just knew what to do, the way she could deal with anything, if there was soup, if there wasn't soup, if she got run down by a bike courier, or if she didn't.

But then there was the streetcar ride. And the orange. Still, I sure knew how nice it would be to have that orange now. Something sweet and juicy. I got up and climbed into the "banquet hall." I checked the seat-shelves but there wasn't much there. In a yoghurt tub, there were some Froot Loops, but I didn't see any milk. Definitely no orange, though I realized now that I probably couldn't have taken it. I didn't find anything I wanted to eat, and, anyway, I wasn't sure I was invited to, exactly. There was an old baseball in a corner, and I took it back out to the "grand foyer." I sat on my unrolled sleeping bag and tossed the ball against the wall, just for something to do.

I must have fallen asleep eventually, because before I knew it, I was waking up to the sound of voices. Moth was climbing in the window, followed by Pilot and two other guys and another girl.

"Look what I found." Moth was calling out, and at first I thought she meant me, but then I saw she was waving a bat. She scooped up the ball I had abandoned on the floor. "Do you play baseball? Let's have a game later."

I thought about my tryout for the school team, a million miles and a thousand years ago. "I've played. I'm not much good."

"Doesn't matter; neither are we. Anybody up for some good, clean fun? By the way, that's Zack and Pete, and that's Slash." So there was a real Zack. "This is Arrow, the guy I told you about. Donna will be here later. I'm starved. Kraft Dinner okay?" Moth was rummaging around a supply box I had missed, pulling out a carton of milk. She sniffed it, swirled the carton and sniffed it again. With a sharp nod, she proclaimed it fit for use and began to clatter out a pot.

It wasn't long before the Coleman stove was lit. Pete stirred the pot. I pulled out my new harmonica and played a note or two. I felt like we were cowboys around a campfire, and it seemed right to have a harmonica.

"Can you play that?" asked Pilot.

"Yeah, really well." I put it up to my mouth and honked out "Old Macdonald." It was terrible and I was out of breath at the end. Everyone laughed. So did I. It was nice.

"It's all in breath control," Pilot said. "Look." He put

out his hand for the harmonica and I passed it over. "See, you've got one note when you breathe out, but in the same place, if you breathe in, you've got another note. Like this." He demonstrated. "If you really learn where they all are, you never have to run out of breath—watch." Pilot played a few bars that sounded like something I thought I'd heard an orchestra play once before. It was amazing. He handed the instrument back to me. "Gershwin. 'Rhapsody in Blue.'"

"Oh," I replied. "I don't know much about music. That was incredible."

Pilot grinned.

"Yes, Pilot's a regular mouth organ virtuoso." It was Pete.

Pilot gave him a dirty look but I wasn't sure why, and then Moth called, with a fake English accent, "Dinnah is sahved."

Soon we were all sitting around the grand foyer, eating Kraft Dinner from a mishmash of plates and bowls. None of the cutlery matched either. I used my own spork, but they had an extra plate for me. I realized it was the first home-cooked dinner—if you could call it that—I'd had since Thursday night. Not that that was really so long ago, but it was long for me. It wasn't much of a meal—there wasn't even anything green, which was good, because in this place that would probably mean mold—but it really was home-cooked. This boat, this collection of street kids, people I might have called homeless if I'd seen them on the street in my old life, were a home. They talked and laughed; they ate together; they seemed to care about each other. It would have been tacos at my old home tonight.

Shredded lettuce would have been the green. As I'd been thinking that morning in the McDonald's, why go on? Here was a home, a place I felt I could be part of, instead of just something like a co-tenant. Here was a place they gave me their Kraft Dinner, though they barely knew me, and asked me to play baseball, and taught me harmonica, instead of getting mad because I made Minute Rice off schedule. And here was a beautiful girl, with magic green eyes, who'd offered me three wishes, and promptly granted the first one by giving me a plan, and she was smiling at me as she took my plate.

We washed the dishes in rainwater from a bucket they kept beside the boat, and then the seven of us walked to a nearby park with the bat and ball. A few teenagers were pitching and hitting on the diamond there, and Pete asked if they wanted to join up for a bit of a game—neither of us had enough for a real game, but if the batting team provided the pitcher and we skipped a shortstop and fielder, we could just manage it. It was past seven o'clock, and I was surprised at how light it still was out, though it looked like it might rain again.

I was actually a better baseball player than any of the others, except maybe Pete. Pilot was not much use; baseball was obviously not his game. He choked the bat way too high, and he looked like it would be emotionally painful if he hit anything and had to run. When it was my turn to bat, I felt oddly nervous. I had to admit it. I wanted to impress Moth. The first pitch hit the dirt in front of me—Ball One. The second was a little outside, but I stupidly swung at it anyway—Strike One. The third pitch was just right, and this time I stood there like an idiot—Strike Two. Moth grinned at me from second base. I took a deep breath.

The ball came toward me and I swung. CR-ACK! I had hit the ball square and hard, and it was sailing high and far. It bounced somewhere behind where a shortstop would have been if we'd had one, and I could see one of the fielders loping back to get the ball he'd missed as I went for second base. I could make it a triple. I passed Moth, who was jumping up and down, and turned toward third, and, just out of the corner of my eye, I saw the fielder pick up the ball. He seemed far away—could I make it? Had I hit a homer? I saw third base, where I could stop and be safe, but I poured on the juice and went on through third. And then I saw the catcher positioning himself for a catch. If the catcher was right in his stance, the throw was dead on. It was exactly the same thing that had happened to me at the tryouts. Clearly not only was I a lousy baseball player, I was dead stupid, too—but there was nothing else to do but barrel on. Then, suddenly, the catcher jumped up, but the ball was way too high, and the next thing I knew, I ran clean into home plate. Moth was still jumping up and down, yelling, even though she was on the other team.

"Woo-hoo! Home run! Way to go—swift as an Arrow from a bow! Hey! I'm a poet!"

And suddenly, it started to rain, hard, and everyone ran for cover under a picnic shelter.

"Well, I guess that's the game," said Pete.

"Arrow hit a home run," sang Moth, as if it was *her*

achievement. She was looking at Pilot, and he said nothing.

"Arrow hit a home run," she sang again, more softly. He looked away.

I liked that she was pleased with me, but I felt uncomfortable with her putting down Pilot. He was probably great at hockey or something. After all, he *was* Canadian.

Moth was still looking at Pilot and she seemed to be about to say something.

"Leave him be," I said quietly. Pilot looked at me but I couldn't read his expression. Was he mad at me now?

"Let's go for a Coke," suggested Donna. "I want to go to a real bathroom." We left the kids we didn't know and ran for a coffee shop across the street. We pulled chairs together around a table and shook the rain out of our hair. Everyone was pretty wet. I noticed again and confirmed that Moth wasn't wearing a bra. Like I said before, I tried to be a gentleman and not stare, but I couldn't help it. A strange pain squeezed my chest. This wasn't like looking at pictures in *Penthouse* magazine with Brian, this was a real girl and I really shouldn't look.

"Oh, my God, look at me," laughed Moth, pulling her white top tight. I thought I'd have a heart attack and die right there. "I'm a wet T-shirt contest! I win!" I swallowed hard and looked down at the table quickly. Things for me were getting a little more like looking at pictures in *Penthouse*.

The Cokes came to the table, and the girls all went off to the washroom, returning in a few minutes, transformed.

Well, Slash looked just the same, but Moth had dried her T-shirt—on the hand-drier, I supposed—and both she and Donna had washed off their makeup.

Without it all, Moth was really beautiful. Her lips were soft and dark pink, and her eyes sparkled like emeralds, with long dark lashes framing them. She looked both wise and innocent. I wished I could kiss her.

"I know," she said, laughing, when she noticed me looking at her, and for a second I thought she had read my mind. "I look awful. But you can't sleep in that stuff. It's bad for your skin."

It was night and very dark in the boat. Everyone was asleep but me, since I'd slept all afternoon. We were all lying next to each other, alternating head to toe. The boys all had their heads to the west, the girls east. The air was thick, but I *had* sort of gotten used to it. It sure beat sleeping under the highway. I could hear the rain on the roof and the lake water slapping the concrete behind the boat. I could hear all the soft breathing, the occasional snort or snore. Now I could make out a small, sharp whimper. Then a little "oh," and a sound like talking but it didn't mean anything. Another "oh," a little louder. It was Moth, who was sleeping beside me, her head at my feet.

I sat up and looked at her. It was very dark and I couldn't see if she was awake. I crawled along my sleeping bag and leaned down to look at her. Her face was troubled, and she shuddered a bit. A nightmare.

I reached out and touched her shoulder. She jumped, then woke up. She looked confused for a moment, half sitting up, then lay back down on her side. Tears rolled out of the corners of her eyes, one across her cheek, the other across her nose. She rubbed that one away.

"Are you okay?" I whispered.

"Bad dreams," Moth muttered, nodding. "I get them ... sometimes."

I lay down, facing Moth. I wished I had a handkerchief for her. I wanted to touch her face, to take her in my arms, to tell her it would all be okay. I wanted to take care of her, like she took care of me today. Her hands were over her eyes—all I could see was her pretty mouth. I wished again I could kiss her. And then I got my second wish.

I wasn't quite sure how it had happened. It was almost just that I willed her to kiss me—well, that was it, of course—it was my second wish, and somehow she knew. Twice she kissed me, not crying any more. And then she curled up on my shoulder like a child and went to sleep.

I couldn't sleep any more that night. Well, except for my left arm, which Moth was lying on, cutting off the circulation. I hoped it wouldn't have to be amputated from lack of blood, but it was almost worth it to have this magical creature nestled next to me. Through one of the portholes above, the one that wasn't broken and covered with cardboard, I could see a patch of sky gradually lightening. The air was almost oxygen-free, the unwashed smell of my bed mates close around me. Some nautical detail was jutting into my back and my left hand was completely numb. But I felt a strange sensation welling up inside of me—a giddiness, a jazziness—something made me want to giggle, as if the back of my throat were being tickled. It took me a while, but gradually I realized what it was. I was happy. I was home. As the sky began to take on that morning glow, Moth rolled over without waking up. I retrieved my arm, which slowly began to prickle and come back to life. I just lay there and smiled.

It turned out it wasn't impossible to shower if you lived on a derelict boat. And since it was already Tuesday morning and I had been traveling through bus stations and other charming scenic spots without a shower since Friday morning, I was grateful for the chance to get clean.

I stepped into the shower and let it run through my hair and over my back. When Moth had woken up in the morning, she had given me a coy smile that was impossible to interpret. Was she embarrassed because she'd cried in front of me, or flirty because we'd kissed? Maybe it was a thank you for taking care of her. Or did she even remember what had happened—did she think it was just a dream? But I knew the boys pointed west, the girls east, and I was pointing east by morning. Did she notice that? Moth never mentioned the nightmare, the tears, the kiss, just bundled up her sleeping bag and said, "I need a shower today." She had brought me to this drop-in center, where there were showers, washing machines, and phones for people to use.

Now, as I lathered up my hair, I even tried to interpret

that remark. Maybe she wanted us both to take showers so either she wouldn't be embarrassed at being dirty if we got close again, or maybe I stank a bit, and she wanted me clean so she could get close. Or maybe I just stank and she was being polite. I rinsed my hair and decided there was no point in trying to speculate, I'd just make myself crazy. Anyway, I heard some rustling outside the shower and that reminded me that my turn was nearly up, so I quickly soaped myself and rinsed off. I wanted to get dressed quickly anyway, in the change of clothes I'd brought with me, because today I was going to get a squeegee and learn my new trade. It wasn't on the list of career choices I had given to Beatrice, but, hey, you never knew where it could lead.

I pulled on my fresh clothes, transferring my wallet to my clean jeans, laced my hiking boots back on, and shoved the dirty clothes back into my pack. It felt incredibly great to be clean. I had not realized how dirty I was—I hadn't even changed my underwear since I left home on Friday morning—until just now.

There were lockers that cost a quarter at the drop-in center, so rather than go all the way back to the boat, we stashed my gear there. Probably safer, anyway. Maybe later I could come back and wash my other clothes.

"Now we'll select your weapon," announced Moth, who looked clean, except that she had all that awful makeup on again. Still, I couldn't miss that sparkle in her eyes. Pilot had arrived and was waiting for us. He glanced at me in what seemed to be a funny way. I wondered again whether

Moth was his girlfriend. They didn't seem to act like they were together, but who knew? Did he know about last night? I kind of smiled at him. Maybe I was just being paranoid. He wasn't much good at baseball, but he was bigger than me.

The three of us walked down the busy street together, and I noticed how hard it was for three people to walk together on a city sidewalk.

"Here," said Moth, as we paused at a store that sold all kinds of plastic things, from sandals to dishes.

"Okay, but I'm *buying* it—no stealing." Moth looked sort of disappointed, but I stuck to my guns. "It's bad luck to steal something you need to do you good." It's just bad to steal was what I was thinking.

"This is the kind you want," said Moth, pointing to the squeegees hanging on the wall in the store. I chose green, for her eyes (though I didn't tell her that), and laid it on the counter. "Twelve sixty-five," the clerk said. Or something. I didn't hear him. I could only stare into my empty wallet. My wallet was completely empty. I felt my stomach drop to my boots.

"Moth. My money. It's all gone. All of it. There was something like seventy dollars in there." I looked at Pilot. I looked at Moth. She was smart. She would know what to do.

But she didn't. "Oh," she said. "Oh."

Leaving the green squeegee on the counter, we trudged out of the store and perched on one of the tree planters. "I thought you said you were broke," Moth finally said.

"I didn't. *You* did."

"You ate our Kraft Dinner. You let us buy you breakfast."

"I would have bought food for the boat. When you bought breakfast, I didn't know I was going to stay. I needed the money for my trip."

"Trip to where?" asked Moth.

Suddenly, I felt cautious about telling her. Or at least cautious with Pilot around.

"I don't know where. I didn't know where I was going. I didn't know I was staying. I don't know!"

"How could you lose seventy dollars?" asked Moth, sounding really upset, almost angry.

"I don't know!" I felt like crying. I tried to think when my wallet had been away from me. At night, while we slept, I'd put it in my pack, but that was right by my head, and anyway I'd been awake for most of the night. And I couldn't imagine that any of them would steal from their own roommate, even if I was new. I remembered the rustling sound I heard while I was in the shower. Well, there were lots of people in the drop-in center, so it could have happened. But that was a pretty nervy thing to do—I could have stepped out at any second and caught the person. Well, it must have been what happened. There was no other explanation.

"So, what do I do now? I can't afford to buy a squeegee, so I can't earn any money." I half hoped that Moth or Pilot would buy it for me. I'd pay them back, of course. But I had a feeling that Moth, at least, was mad at me for losing so much money.

"What about a bank card?" she asked suddenly.

"A bank card?"

"Yeah, do you have any money in an account, or could you get a cash advance, or something?"

I unfolded my wallet. My bank card, student card, library card, and a few others were all still there. It was strange to see them, with my old address—the video store card —and now I didn't even have a VCR.

"You know, I did leave twenty bucks in my account, for appearances, when I took my money out. But I can't touch it. If I do, they'll know where I am."

There was silence for a moment.

"They'll know where the card is. They don't have proof you're with it."

"Sure they do. They have video cameras at those bank machines." And the last thing I needed was for my father to figure out I was so close to Kingston. Then he'd know for sure and might even try to find me before I got there, even though I wasn't going now. Yes, that's what he would do, I knew it now. If he figured out where I was going, he'd try to intercept me and steal me again. The thought made me feel sick. I'd still have to go back to live with my father, after I'd turned my back on him forever—or for a long time, anyway.

"It's your only choice, though," Moth almost pleaded. "I know! Tell me your code and I'll go. At least they won't see you. They won't know for sure."

It seemed clear that I wasn't getting a squeegee from Moth, though I wasn't sure what was different about today, when I didn't have any money, and yesterday when she *thought* I didn't have any money.

I looked at Pilot to see if I might score any help there, but he only looked at the ground, swinging the end of the squeegee between his feet, which, unlike mine, reached the ground from the planter.

"I guess it's my only chance." I wished I could think of something, *anything* else. I didn't like this plan one bit. It just exposed me way too much. But there was no other choice. "One-one-oh-eight," I told her, handing the card over. "It's my birthday."

"Which way round?" Moth thought a moment. "Leo or Scorpio?"

"Uh ... Leo."

Moth looked thoughtfully at me. "Funny, I wouldn't have guessed either one. Pisces, maybe. Or Libra. You must have afflictions in your chart."

Afflictions. She got that right. I just shrugged my shoulders.

Since rush hour was slipping away, Moth and Pilot said they'd do some cars first, then meet me at the boat for a coffee break, with the money. I set off for the drop-in center to get my backpack before heading for home.

"I'll bring you a coffee," Moth called after me. "How do you take it?"

"Black," I called over my shoulder. It would match my mood.

I had no thoughts but gloom as I sat and waited for Pilot and Moth's return. How could I have been so stupid as to leave my wallet so easily found? How could I have lost so much money? It was the stolen streetcar ride, I was sure of it. Every time I stole a ride, I lost my money. Never, never, never again. Not that I was going anywhere. And now my dad would probably find me and make me go back. I glanced at the name *Coleman* on the stove. Back or forward? But I wasn't going anywhere. I wasn't going to move.

Finally, I heard footsteps on the concrete. Now my money would arrive, I could buy a squeegee, and my new life could begin. I started to feel a tiny bit better.

Pilot clambered onto the boat but he seemed to be alone.

"Where's Moth?"

"Oh, uh ..." Pilot looked around the grand foyer like he was looking for something, but he didn't seem to find it, and then sat down on a wooden box.

"She stopped for coffee?" I guessed.

"Yeah, that's right."

Pilot was acting so weird I decided he must be Moth's boyfriend. Maybe he knew about the kiss. Maybe Moth had sent him back alone to beat me up or something. (*No, come on, that's ridiculous. Well, what, then?*)

"Is Moth your girlfriend?" I finally asked. I had to know.

"No-oh." Pilot half snorted. "No, I don't have a girlfriend. Moth doesn't have a boyfriend, either. But I don't recommend you auditioning for the part."

"Why not?"

"She's just a teensy bit unreliable," said Pilot. Obviously the understatement of the year. Well, I had kind of figured, but that was part of her charm.

We were both silent for a while.

"She's sure taking her time with that coffee."

Pilot looked straight at me and I knew what he was going to say before he said it.

"She's not bringing coffee. She's not bringing money, either. She's not coming back."

Even though I had known it, hearing it nearly knocked me over. "Not ever?"

"Oh, she'll be back. After you give up waiting for her."

"For twenty doll—" And then I knew the rest.

"All of it," said Pilot.

"Did she tell you she took it?" This can't be right, it *can't*.

"No." *There! Aha! Aha!* "She didn't have to. I know Moth."

That's not proof! "That's not proof!" I was desperate.

"Trust me. Moth can smell money and she can find it. A Twinkie like you always has money."

"What's a Twinkie?" I had to ask, even though I was pretty sure it was an insult.

"See? A Twinkie is a new kid, a kid who goes home to Daddy and Mommy at night. A kid who's here on a lark."

"I'm not here on a lark!" This was unfair.

"No, but you're new. And unless you get a tougher center, you won't last."

"But how do you know for sure it was Moth who took my money? It could have been anyone in the shower."

"Because that's what she does," said Pilot with a tired sigh.

"Come on, I could easily have looked out of the shower. What would she have said then?"

"Moth? She probably would have taken off all her clothes and gotten in the shower with you. She would have done anything. Tried for the money again later. How do you think she knew you had a bank card?"

The image of Moth in the shower with me made my mind reel. But Pilot seemed to really know her. It all had the ring of truth. Yet, still, I tried to find the place where it was wrong, where it was a lie, a mistake. "Well, why are you telling me this? Aren't you her friend? Won't you get your share of the money? Shouldn't I just wait and get in on it?"

Pilot shook his head. "I won't get any money. I just think you're a nice guy and you deserve to know."

"Why won't you get the money? What will she spend it on? Kraft Dinner and stuff. Peanut butter."

"Makeup. Tattoos. Grass. Cocaine. Whatever's around. Whatever's fun." *Cocaine?* "Now I want to know something. You were going somewhere when you got here. Not here."

I thought a moment before answering. I still wasn't sure I trusted Pilot. "What makes you say that?"

"Well, you sort of said it. You said you didn't know in McDonald's that you were going to stay."

"I didn't know where I was going."

Pilot looked at me. He was waiting for the truth. "Americans don't run away to Toronto," he pointed out. "Too risky." I must have look like I didn't understand. "Crossing the border," he said.

"A relative. I can't say anything else."

"You're looking for someone."

I nodded slowly. "I don't want to tell you more. With that

card used, they might look for me here. If you don't know, you can't tell them."

"Fair enough," said Pilot. "I think you should go there. I think you should stop playing house here and find whatever it is you're looking for."

"How can I? I don't have a red cent. I can't get anywhere. Even if I walked, I'd need food."

Pilot thought a moment. "Wait here," he said and left the boat.

While I waited for Pilot to return, I tried practicing my harmonica the way he had showed me, and I could almost sort of play "Old MacDonald" now. Maybe I could earn money as a busker. Stay here and outwait Moth, live on the yacht. Yeah, in my dreams, maybe.

Finally, I gave up on Pilot ever coming back and began trying to work out the moral implications of selling the Coleman stove. Would it really be stealing, or just getting something back for the money Moth had taken? But I knew, I knew in my heart that it would be stealing, because Moth wasn't the only one who lived here. It would be stealing from Slash and Zack and Pete and Donna, who'd done nothing to me. It would be stealing from Pilot, though I wasn't so sure he wasn't this moment in the process of stealing from me. And it wasn't like I could send the money back later. What would I write on the envelope: "Pilot, The Yacht, Toronto"? I just wished I could think of a way to get out of here.

I had moved onto the possibility of pawning the harmonica, but I didn't really know how pawnshops worked or where I could find them, or if they even existed outside the comics, when I heard footsteps again. Pilot climbed onto the boat, and he didn't look happy.

"Sorry I took so long. Here."

It was two of the purple ones and a blue one. Twenty-five dollars.

"I can't ..." I started, but I could, I could. Taking a gift wasn't stealing.

"You have to. It's your only choice." I knew it was true.

"Where did you get it?"

"You don't want to know."

"But—"

Pilot cut me off. "No, you *don't... want... to know.* It's not stolen, if that's what you're worried about."

I looked at Pilot. Something, though I didn't know what it was, told me to leave it alone. I probably *didn't* want to know.

"Thanks, man. Is there some place I can send it back to? Can I pay you back?"

"I'll make *her* pay me back." Pilot grinned.

I slipped my "mouth organ," as Pete had called it, into my pocket and hoisted my pack onto my shoulder. Most of me couldn't wait to get out of there, but one little part of me actually didn't want to go. I wanted it all to have been true.

"Don't take it personally. It's just what she does. She liked you. She told me. I like you, too." He pointed to the chest pocket of my jean jacket where my harmonica was. "Practice that harp—breath control. And take care."

I couldn't think of anything to say, so I punched Pilot on his tattoo.

"Hey, man, don't, you're gonna make me cry." He was kidding, of course.

"Bye, Pilot—thanks for everything." I climbed off the boat and started away.

"Bye, Arrow. Fall to earth someplace cool."

I couldn't look back but I raised my hand in a salute of goodbye.

I was back in the bus station, on the phone, breathing in diesel again, trying to be invisible. Now that my bank card had been used in Toronto, I knew that if the police were looking for me, they would soon find me here. And the bus station was just the kind of place they'd look. A soupy male voice over the phone was saying "... press threee. For student fares, press fourrr ..." I pressed four.

"The one-way student fare from To-ront!-to to K-I-N-G-S-T-O-N is ... sixty-six ninety—" I hung up on the recorded message. I felt sick. So far today, I'd had nothing to eat or even more than water to drink. I had to get out of Toronto, and fast. I didn't dare run the risk of hitchhiking—I'd be sure to be picked up by a cop—now that they could be looking for me, and looking in the right place, too. I went out to where the buses were waiting for passengers and sat down. I pulled out my fairly dog-eared map and tried to think what to do. Could there be another city in the same direction, maybe one that was twenty-five dollars away? I could figure out how to get the forty-one dollars further when I got there. At least I'd be away from Toronto.

Under the map, there was a somewhat misshapen chocolate bar, one of the last three from the ones I'd bought from Paula. This Saturday was Paula's party. I wondered if Brian would go. It all seemed so distant, like another world. I realized that I must have been missed from school by now—it was Tuesday. I wondered if Paula noticed. I was hardly ever away from school, since I'm practically never sick, so for me to be away for two days might make people wonder. Or maybe people knew I was gone. I still couldn't decide for sure whether my father would have called the police, but now I thought he probably would have had to. Once he'd spoken to Brian's father, Brian's father would know I was gone, so he would have had to act normal, and normal was calling the police. Unless he'd noticed the picture was missing. Then he'd know. I felt sicker.

The chocolate bar wasn't much of a breakfast, but I couldn't afford to part with any of Pilot's money until I knew what I was going to do. On the map, I saw that Belleville was the next closest big place to Kingston—it looked to be about forty or fifty miles from there. I went back inside and called the bus station from itself again. It seemed weird, but I didn't want to draw attention to myself by going up to the counter over and over. At least Moth had so kindly left me the change in my pockets. I felt a flash of anger, and I wasn't so sure I wasn't madder at myself for being so stupid than at her.

Amazingly, the one-way student ticket to Belleville was only $27.50, which didn't make any sense, since it was most of the way to Kingston, but I pressed the star key to hear the message again, and it seemed to be right. I dug through my pockets and pack, but only found sixty cents, so I still needed a dollar ninety and, even then, I wouldn't get anything to eat. And I'd need to have some money for after Belleville, because I'd still be fifty miles away from my goal. And even when I got to Kingston, who knew what would happen next?

A trickle of nerves ran down my throat to my stomach. *When I got to Kingston.* Suddenly, I was facing what I had done, what I was doing, and I was scared. *Who knew what would happen next?*

I stepped out of the bus station, the opposite way to the way I had gone the first night. There seemed to be a busy street and a shopping mall that way, and I started in that direction. When I got to the major street, it was crazy busy. Not just cars and pedestrians and cyclists, but a ticket booth, a guy selling hot dogs, a guy on one of those old-folks scooters covered in signs, ringing a bell. There was a guitarist singing and playing for money (and he looked like he had a lot in his guitar case, too). A couple of kids that looked like they might know Moth and Pilot, huddled together as if they were cold, with dead-white skin, staring ahead with blank eyes. Two teenaged girls, giggling too loud, smoking cigarettes. Shouldn't they be in school? Somebody walking by the guitar guy dropped a heavy-sounding coin in his case. Probably a dollar coin, the one they called a "loonie," of all things. Two of those and I could buy my ticket. And that was when I got my idea.

I crossed the street to be away from the guitar player.

I tore a poster off a lamppost it had been taped to and fished in my bag for Beatrice's pen. I wrote BUS MONEY in big outline letters on the paper, and colored them in a little with diagonal lines so people could see them. With my Rangers cap on the sidewalk in front of me, the sign taped to it with a bit of the tape from the poster, I pulled out Claire's harmonica.

I began playing "Old MacDonald." I was doing not too badly. Okay, actually, I was pretty bad, missed the timing a bit, but got most of the notes, except for the one where there would have been the word "duck" or something. It came out a bit quack-like. I pressed on. "With a—" and that's when I became brilliant. I did the "quack" notes on the "quack-quack here" part. A lady walking by smiled and dropped a quarter into my hat. I nodded my thanks.

I played it again. This time, I tried to make a low "moo" sound in the proper places. I got fifty more cents. All right!

Round and round I played the same song, over and over, trying different funny sounds. I got better and better as I went, finding the notes, controlling my breathing. Nickels, quarters, a few pennies, one loonie. After almost an hour, I was pretty exhausted and I paused, glancing into my hat. There weren't that many coins in the hat, but to me, it looked like pirate's treasure. I counted it. Ten dollars and ninety-three cents. Enough for the bus ticket and—quick calculation with Beatrice's pen—and nine dollars and three cents left over. So I could get to Belleville. And I could eat. Thank you, Claire.

The bus didn't go until early afternoon, and I was so hungry I thought I'd puke if I didn't eat, so I went into the shopping mall. There was bound to be a food court, and they usually had something cheap.

I ended up with a bagel and cream cheese and a glass of water—a real no-color lunch that cost me $1.80 ($7.23 left), though at least there was a piece of pickle with it. I wondered if it counted as something green, but I really didn't care. I just wanted to get on that bus to Belleville and out of Toronto.

There were a lot of teenagers hanging around the food court and they were nothing like Moth and her friends, so I realized maybe Toronto wasn't as weird as I had thought. These were regular kids, probably on lunch from some nearby high school, wearing team jackets and baseball hats, regular jeans and T-shirts. Anyone just looking at me wouldn't even know I wasn't just some ordinary local kid. Except that I looked at my watch every twenty-three seconds. Finally, it was time to get the bus.

I bought my own ticket this time, in spite of the chance of being recognized if they came looking for me. There was no way I was trusting my precious money out of my sight for a second.

I really hoped no one would sit beside me—I just couldn't face making up some story for some new person, holding all the details in my head, and, for once, I got my wish. I smiled—sort of. Maybe Moth had granted my third wish after all.

The bus pulled out without me having been clapped in

irons (who was I—Long John Silver?), and I finally relaxed a little. The little bit of a high I was on after earning my bus fare on my own had worn off as I realized I was still really in a jam. I thought about Moth. And Pilot. And the money. And everything that had happened. I felt so confused. Had Moth set out to rob me, right from the beginning? It seemed like it, if Pilot was telling the truth. And why wouldn't Pilot tell the truth? So what was real and what was fake? Her cheering me on at the baseball game, the crying, the kiss, the welcome to live on the boat, buying the squeegee—which, I now realized, had to have been an act because she *knew* I didn't have the money any more. And yet, Pilot said she liked me—so why would she do a thing like that to me? And what about Pilot? How much had he known all along? And how on earth could he have found $25 and not want me to know how if it wasn't stolen? Maybe he sold something. Probably.

Oh, what was the use in going over this? Everything was a mess. I was practically out of money, with a ticket only partway to where I was going, no plan, the police almost certainly aware of where I was. If only there was some way I could find out what was going on at home, call Brian or something. But if the police were involved, they'd have the lines traced for sure. And how was I going to get from Belleville to Kingston?

It was exhausting, and I hadn't slept much last night. As the city slipped away behind us, as I started to slide into sleep, I suddenly had the answer. I had slept through Indianapolis and I hadn't got caught. I could just "sleep" through Belleville—Kingston was bound to be the next stop.

Yeah, yeah, I hadn't forgotten. Every time I stole a ride, I lost my money. But this time, I wasn't letting the money out of my sight. And, yes, I also knew it was wrong to steal. But I couldn't help it. It wasn't like Moth. Was it?

I turned my mind away from the thought and fell asleep.

Napanee, according to my map, was only twenty or so miles from Kingston. That was the good news. The bad news was that I was no longer on the bus. I was on a highway off-ramp cut out of a gray, rocky landscape. There was no point in hitchhiking—it was after seven o'clock and it would soon be getting dark. And I wasn't booted off at a real bus stop, so I doubted there would be a bus from this little place, even if I had the money for a ticket.

As I expected, the bus had pulled in at Belleville. I wasn't asleep, so I just tried to keep still, tried to look angelic and relaxed. A few people got off and on, but no one bothered me and no one sat next to me on this leg, either.

About forty minutes later, the bus pulled off the highway. We were in Kingston already? I started to get my stuff organized, but then the bus stopped and the driver got out of his seat and ambled back to mine.

"See your ticket, son?"

My heart went cold. I pulled the ticket out of my jacket pocket and handed it over, as if I were completely innocent.

"That's what I thought."

"What?"

"Your ticket is for Belleville."

"Yeah. Belleville."

"Belleville is back that way."

"It is? Oh, no! I guess I slept through it." I looked out the window. It was clearly not a real bus stop. "Uh, I guess I'll have to go back from, uh, where's next? Kingston?"

"How old are you?"

"Sixteen."

The driver shook his head. "Tell you what, kid, cross to the other side of the highway, and I'll radio the next bus from Kingston to pick you up and take you back."

"Oh, you don't have to do that! I'll just go back from Kingston."

"You'd have to buy another ticket. Just go on, kid. It's no problem. See? Just follow the road and wait on the on-ramp. The bus will pass by in about half an hour."

There was nothing I could think of to say. Here was this guy being *nice* to me when *I* was trying to steal a ride from him.

We learned about irony in English this year. I was pretty sure this was it.

And now, here I was, stranded twenty miles from my destination.

Twenty miles. I could walk. It seemed like the only safe and sensible thing to do, and twenty miles was a long way but it wasn't impossible. I would go as far as I could tonight, and tomorrow—

Tomorrow! I would be in Kingston tomorrow! My mind swirled at the thought. Just as well I was going to walk. I needed time to think.

I walked in the direction I assumed the lake would be. Kingston was on that huge lake, the same one as Toronto, Lake Ontario. I figured if I found a major road going east-west, I could probably follow it into town. My map didn't have enough detail to be clear exactly where I should go. But taking the side roads seemed saner than trying to follow the four-lane highway, and less attention-provoking.

It wasn't long before I did find a major-enough looking road and I turned left. Soon, I was out of the town and into farmland. The sun was getting low and I was starving. Time to start thinking about dinner and a bed.

But there was nothing but farm after farm. It was too early for any crops—I couldn't steal carrots or even strawberries. In Texas, I might have found some food growing, but up north here, there was nothing to eat this early. And even though it had been a warm day, I remembered from the boat, and, worse, under the highway, how cold it got around here at night. Maybe a barn would give me a bit of shelter. It looked like dinner would be Paula's last chocolate bars, but I would probably be able to find a place for breakfast, and I could probably even afford something decent with the money I had left. I figured breakfast was more important with a long walk ahead than dinner was before a night's sleep.

A likely-looking barn was looming up on the left, green with white trim. By keeping low among the long grass and circling around, I made it into the barn without being seen from the house. Inside the barn, it smelled of hay and cows. And, well, what hay is after it's been through cows. There were some cows in the barn, which seemed odd to me since, in Texas, the cattle roam the range, mostly. But of course, those were beef cattle, and these ones would have to be milked in the morning. I looked at the udders and wondered if there was any way I could get a drink of milk from them, but since I didn't have the first clue how to milk a cow, and none of them were offering, I decided I'd have to do without.

There was no one in the barn, but I went up into the hayloft where I would be more out of sight, especially in case I didn't wake up early enough to be gone before the farmer might come to milk the cows. The hayloft was perfect. It was a little warmer and the air was fresher. It was kind of cozy, knowing the cows were down there for company. I made myself a little bed of hay, with a pile shielding my stuff from view of the ladder, in case anyone came up. Later, I would lay out my sleeping bag but, right now, I had to devour those last chocolate bars.

It wasn't enough. Oh, it wasn't close to enough. All the chocolate bars did was remind me I had a stomach, and it made me feel like I was going to throw up. I *had* to get something more to eat.

I wondered if there was any way I could get some food from the farmhouse. I doubted it would be a good idea just to walk up to the door and ask. But maybe, out here, people didn't lock their doors or close their windows all the way.

Maybe, after the people had gone to bed—and they'd have to go to bed early if they were getting up to milk cows ... I decided to see if I could at least find a place where I could watch the house without being seen. I headed for the ladder but, just before I descended, some instinct told me to bring my pack with me. Being separated from my stuff just didn't feel like a good idea at all.

Soon, I had a place in the bushes at the back of the house, next to a chicken house. It was quiet but noisy. It was all that calm of night away from the city, but the air was also filled with the sounds of slow crickets, small rustlings, a frog or two, an owl, and the chickens occasionally moving around in their coop. Oh, and the buzz of mosquitoes that kept landing on me. I kept brushing them away but couldn't slap at them because I didn't want to make any noise. There was a little light leaking through from the front of the house—maybe the people were in the living room, watching TV or something. This was way too risky. I couldn't even try to get something to eat until everyone in the house was in bed asleep. And anyway, my conscience was gnawing at me. (At least some part of me was getting a good meal!) I couldn't break into someone's house and steal food. I'd done plenty of borderline things since I'd left Dallas on Saturday, but this wasn't borderline. These were real people, probably not even rich. And I wasn't going to starve to death in a night—people in faraway countries starve for days or more before they die. I was still hungry, but I picked up my pack and started creeping back to the barn. Stooped down with my pack on my back, I scrambled across the small open patch between the bushes and the barn. Luckily, it was quite dark away from the house.

Suddenly, a flash, a loud bang, and a sharp sting, like a whip, hit the back of my hand. Another flash and bang, but no sting. I dashed, crouching low behind the barn on the side away from the house, then straightened up and ran blindly into the woods.

Stumbling through roots and long grass, I felt my way in the dark and down a small bank. Behind me, I could hear an angry voice, a little swearing, and the word "coyote"—the farmer pronounced it "kye-OH-tee," not "KYE-oat," like we do in Texas. I guess the guy figured I was an animal after his chickens. My hand hurt like fire.

When I figured I was far enough away, but before I got totally lost in the woods, I stopped. There was a rock next to a tree that looked like an okay place to sit. My eyes had gotten used to the dark, so I could see surprisingly well, especially since there was a close-to-full moon out. That was an interesting thing. In books I've read, people always had a full moon when they needed to be able to see by night, and I always thought it seemed ridiculous because the moon doesn't really give that much light. But now that I was out in the country, away from the street-lit suburbs, I saw it was really true that the moon gave light.

To examine my wound, though, I pulled out my flashlight. I was glad that I had packed some camping stuff. I licked the blood away to see how bad my hand was. Luckily, it seemed to be just grazed, though it was still bleeding. I found my dirty T-shirt in my pack and wrapped it firmly around my hand for pressure and to soak up the blood.

I didn't really like the idea of spending the night in the woods, but there just wasn't any other choice. I couldn't quite use my left hand, so it was awkward, but I managed to undo my sleeping bag and I sat on the rock, pulling the sleeping bag around me like a robe. It was hard, but at least it wasn't damp like the ground would be. With my pack by my head as a sort of pillow, I made myself as comfortable as I could. I couldn't see any house lights, so I figured I was safe from view in the morning, though I knew I wouldn't get any sleep at all in such an uncomfortable and vaguely dangerous place. But when I tried to begin sorting things out in my head, my brain turned into compost and I fell into a dark cloud of sleep.

It was dark everywhere around, with shadowy shapes that could have been trees, rocks, or lurking animals. Strange rustlings and sounds I didn't know what to make of were everywhere, and it was hard to see whether things were moving or if it was just a trick of my mind. Suddenly, one of the shapes I was sure was a rock began to move. Slowly, at first, it was inching toward me. I tried to run, but found that my feet were stuck in boggy ground. The shape was getting closer, moving faster, and I struggled harder and harder with the bog, but I seemed to sink deeper. The shape, which seemed now to be a coyote, suddenly leapt for me, and I jumped as hard as I could, leaping free from the nightmare. But a split second before I woke, the coyote's face had suddenly become my father's.

My heart was racing as I woke up, but the surroundings were so similar to the nightmare, at first I wasn't sure if I had really woken up. I calmed down gradually, though, when I could see that there was no coyote and it was much less dark than the dream, but I still felt uneasy.

In the real world, birds began yelling. The night became gradually less dark, turning into an overcast dawn. I was cold and horribly stiff. My hand was particularly stiff— the same arm that had woken up asleep under Moth just yesterday—and I was still clutching the T-shirt around it. First things first. I unwrapped the T-shirt and slowly unclenched my fist. Of course, this opened the wound again and it bled a little. I stared at my hand, watching the blood appear slowly in the gash. It wasn't a very bad cut, so I was lucky. But I knew I would never steal another ride in my life. The first two times, I only lost my money; I never figured on getting shot for it. I suddenly realized I could have been killed, which was a frightening thought. A few inches west and I would have been toast.

But my hand was sort of fine. I wrapped the T-shirt around it again and started to take stock. It was obviously very early, but I had at least fifteen miles still to go, so I reckoned I might as well get started. I thought if I walked about three miles an hour—a slow estimate, but probably a realistic one—I'd be in Kingston in six hours, say, around early afternoon, which would give me a little time to start figuring out what to do next. Also, I was starving, stiff, and sick. I needed food and I needed to move. Time to go.

I could see the house and barn once I climbed up on the little bank I'd come down the night before, so I kept very low and very far away from them until I was actually on the road. I wasn't sorry to leave that place behind.

I had been walking an hour, taking a turn or two when the road ran out, and I still hadn't come to a place to get something to eat. Had these people never heard of McDonald's, or even just a diner? But that was just it, "these people" was mostly farms, too spread out for anyone to open a restaurant around. It would have been an easy drive to a town for them but I didn't have a vehicle. I was feeling weak, even shaky, when I finally came upon a little place, kind of a diner. I pushed open the door and nearly cried when I smelled the eggs and bacon cooking. I dropped into a booth and pulled the menu from behind the napkin dispenser. Bacon, eggs, hash browns, toast, juice, coffee: $2.95. Yes!

The waitress looked at me kind of funny when she took my order, but she didn't say anything. When I saw myself in the washroom mirror, I could see why—I had a few dried blood spots on my T-shirt, along with dirty smears on my clothes and face, and there was a piece of hay in my hair and dead leaves and stuff from the forest on my shoulder. I looked like I'd slept in my clothes—which I had—and I looked pale and tired. You'd never have guessed I'd had a shower and put on fresh clothes just the day before.

I washed my face, combed my hair with my fingers, and fixed my clothes as well as I could, and, when I returned to the table, the best meal I had ever had in my life arrived. The eggs, scrambled, were rich and sunshine-tasting, and the bacon made my taste buds cry. One bite of my toast, white, and I was in the middle of a wheat field. A sip of my juice, canned, transported me to a golden Florida grove. I hadn't known it was possible to make hash browns this good, to make any food this good. And even though it would only leave me $1.33, I ordered it all again.

While I was waiting for my second breakfast, I pulled a napkin out of the dispenser. I thought I might start writing a letter to Brian. I reached into my pack for Beatrice's pen, and I also took out Claire's harmonica. As I was pulling them from the front pocket, I felt something hard in the main part of my pack that I couldn't identify.

I dug in there and, even before I pulled it out, I knew it by feel. It was a baseball. It was the same make as the one on Moth and Pilot's boat. In fact, it was the same ball, I was sure of it. I remembered my home run that night and the tradition of getting to keep a home run ball. I looked at it from all sides. I was sure it was my home run ball, but I had no idea how it had gotten into my pack. I set it on the table beside the pen and the harmonica. My second breakfast came then.

"You're a baseball fan?" asked the waitress.

"Yeah, kind of."

"My kids are all into that these days, with the Blue Jays doing so well and all."

"It's a good game. I like Tom Henke."

The waitress smiled at me. "Joe Carter, that's my

man." She refilled my coffee cup and went off.

As I ate, I tried to think what I would say to Brian, but I couldn't, not yet. I'd had the craziest trip, but it wasn't over and, until it was, I really didn't know what to make of it all. I just stared at the three things—the pen, the harmonica, the baseball—as if they were some kind of especially challenging question on an exam.

The waitress was nice—she only charged me two-fifty for the second breakfast. "The coffee's a bottomless cup, honey," she told me. Just as well, too, because I forgot to allow for tax and a tip. The bill came to $6.27. I left fifty cents for a tip, which was kind of cheap but it was all I could afford. I picked up the harmonica and the pen and stashed them back in my pack. I touched the baseball, my home run ball, and then, at the last second, I left it there. Maybe the waitress's kids would enjoy it.

With the few coins left in my pocket, I had exactly one dollar and six cents left. But I was full and my strength came back, and I was ready to walk the rest of the way to meet my fate. And besides, I had my harmonica. And I could play "Old Macdonald."

The weather was nice—sunny, not too hot, so the walk would be okay. Nobody seemed to pay much attention to me, though I didn't meet too many people on foot.

After an hour or so of walking toward Kingston, a building with towers came into view on the right—probably some sort of theme park, because it looked like a castle. As I got closer, though, I saw high fences topped with barbed wire and I realized it must be a jail. The castle's turrets were really watchtowers. It somehow seemed appropriate, after all the dishonest things I'd done on this journey.

I thought of how far I'd come across my Formica-topped desk. I wondered how quickly my father would get rid of it, like he had with Rover's leash and stuff. And then it clicked. He *did* already know he wasn't coming back. Rover never ran away. My father had stolen him from me.

Out of nowhere, an enormous wave of rage washed over me, the one I'd been holding back, turning away from, all across the continent. Here I was, walking down a road with no sidewalks, in a foreign country, broke, dirty, exhausted, bloody and with a bullet wound, homeless, basically an orphan, footsore, and, yes, scared. And why? Because of my father. Because Rover wasn't the only thing he'd stolen. My father had stolen *me*. Stolen my mother from me. Stolen my past from me. Stolen the truth from me. And in the end, stolen my father from me. Because who was my father? I had no idea. The man who had raised me to be honest, to be upright and principled and true? The man who had insisted on me being the kind of person I was— a person who cared about what was right—was the worst liar and thief and sham in the world. And where, before, this kind of thinking had just made me confused, now it made me overwhelmingly angry. I didn't know where I was going. I didn't know why I'd made this trek. Who was my mother, either? And I might have done a couple of sort of wrong things, but I wasn't Moth or that Cam Taylor who stole all my money. And I wasn't my father, either, who had stolen me, lied to me, and I couldn't even begin to imagine what he'd done to my mother, still looking for me all these years later. And so here I was. Lost and angry, in front of the jail that looked like a castle, I flung down my pack, sat on it, and cried until there was nothing left in me.

The trouble with crying like that, I discovered, is that unless you've cried yourself to sleep, there comes a point where you realize you have to stop, and you do, and then you feel stupid, and you wonder if anyone saw you. So I stood up, shouldered my pack, wiped my face with the sleeve of my jacket, and started walking again. Toward Kingston, toward whatever would be there.

The jail slowly disappeared behind me as I walked on, but it never really became countryside again. It seemed like I was on the outskirts of Kingston and, eventually, I passed one of those signs that tell you there are Rotary Clubs, Kiwanis, Scouts, and other stuff in town, and here I was. And there was a cop car past the next light. It might not be for me, but I wasn't taking any chances, so I turned away from the lake and began looking for a different east-west street, which I soon found, and started walking along it.

The next thing I had to do was find my mother. The obvious thing to do was check the phone book, though it didn't seem likely it would be that easy. I began to keep a lookout for a phone booth with a book. The first two had no books but, after a while, I saw a shopping mall ahead. I walked on, across the wide parking lot, and into the mall, and went straight for the bank of phones near the door. I flipped open the slim phone book. I tried Ramsay but, though there were several Ramsays, there was no Y. Ramsay. It was lucky my mother had the unusual name of Yvonne. There was nothing under "Coleman," but then I realized I wasn't looking under the "Kingston" heading. I flipped the pages over to Kingston, and then I stopped, suddenly scared.

What if she wasn't in the phone book?

Or worse—what if she was? I felt a little nauseous.

She was. Well, a *Y. Coleman*, anyway, and how many first names start with a Y? Yolanda, Yves, Yvonne. Maybe a couple of others. Not the most common names in the world. Y. Coleman lived on Chestnut Street. That sounded like a nice street. Yes. I realized I was thinking these inane thoughts because I had no idea what to think, and I definitely didn't want to deal with what I felt. *Scared, scared, scared. Don't pay any attention.* All I had to do was phone—or just go to Chestnut Street. That made more sense. Just go to Chestnut Street. And I would. I'd write down the number—388—and then I would go to Y. Coleman's house on Chestnut Street. That's right.

I probably would have stood there until I grew a beard as long as ZZ Top's, if some guy hadn't asked me if I was done with the phone.

"Of course." I stepped aside. I felt cold, cold, shaky, needed some food, needed to lie down somewhere and wake up—later—maybe somewhere else. I had a dollar and six cents. Enough for the smallest McDonald's hamburger. And then that would be it. I might have a penny for luck.

But how could I just go over to Y. Coleman's house on Chestnut Street? First of all, it probably wasn't even her. She could have married again and changed her name, or moved away, or anything. But then I remembered what I'd said to Brian when he put out all those same objections. She'd stay put, where I could find her, just like when you went to the mall with your dad, or I suppose, your mom, or the fair with Brian's folks and they would say, "If you lose me, you just stay where you saw me last. I'll come and find you."

I'll come and find you.

I'll come and find you, Mom, I'll come and find you.

And so I went to the information booth in the mall, and they showed me where Chestnut Street was—a long walk, but possible, I knew, after the last sixteen hundred miles, and I got the smallest McDonald's hamburger, and I didn't lie down somewhere—I just walked.

I kept remembering that country song, "Keep on putting one foot down in front of the other." I was getting a blister on my heel. The country tune twanged in my head as I passed strip malls and muffler shops. It looked a bit like home. Former home. I passed another, smaller, older shopping mall. "Walk on Faith," that was the name of the song.

Past some stores, some motels. The buildings here were

older and the trees bigger than at home, tall as cotton-woods, but more of them. My wounded hand throbbed. The blister was getting worse—it was hard to keep my heel away from the rubbing part. I figured it must be swelling up.

I checked my hand-drawn map. I was looking for a street called Division Street, where I was supposed to turn left. The buildings here were old and the streets set at odd angles to each other. The grass was scruffy.

I turned again, and then again, and looked for the number of Y. Coleman's house on Chestnut Street—388. The street was nice enough, but not the kind of street I'd expected with a name like Chestnut Street. There were some cars parked at the edge of the road, and it was both newer and older than I was expecting. Some of the houses were very old, a hundred years old, maybe, or more, like on the other streets nearby, but others were not so old at all. Like, old, but not as old—boring-old instead of historic-old, including the boxy apartment building with the number 388 on the front—the number I was looking for. Y. Coleman's house on Chestnut Street.

I stopped and looked up at the building.

"Chris."

I froze. *Who knew me?* I whipped around to see an unfamiliar car, passenger door held open—by my father. I felt like I'd been stabbed with an icicle. It was my nightmare, alive.

"Come on, son, hop in." His voice was gentle, warm, not angry like I was expecting.

I could hardly breathe, much less think. After a moment, I shook my head.

"Come on, we have to get going."

Finally, I found my voice. "I'm not going anywhere." Not sullen, just a statement of fact.

"What's the problem, son?"

"You should have told me. You lied to me. You should have told me."

My father sighed and looked like he made a little decision. "You found the picture, I noticed. I'm sorry, Chris. You were too young to understand. It was a grown-ups' situation. You'll be sixteen in August, and I was going to explain it to you then." He gave me a sad smile. "Kids! You grow up so fast these days." He shook his head. *Idon'tknowIdon'tknowIdon'tknow.* It all looked good, but I didn't know if I trusted it.

"Look," he went on. "I can explain, but it's very complicated. Just hop in and we'll go to the hotel, get room service, and I'll lay it all out for you."

It sounded okay, I wanted it to be all right but, still, I didn't trust it. "Explain here, now."

"Chris ..." It had a note of long-suffering patience that sounded more familiar to me.

"Explain here, now." I swallowed. I couldn't quite get

my breath and I couldn't quite connect to my own body. I couldn't believe I was ordering my father.

"You don't know your mother. She's not whatever you've magically dreamed up in your imagination."

A war was going on in my head. He could be right; he could be telling me the truth. I knew less about my mother than I did about him. But something in me didn't trust him. Look where trusting got me on this strange journey, any-way—Cam, Moth. But I trusted Beatrice, I trusted Claire's family, and those turned out well.

"I know you're probably thinking of the court ruling."

Yeah! That's right, he's right, a court ruling must have put me with her! I never thought of that!

"But there was a reason we split, and a reason you need-ed to be with me, in spite of the ruling."

That's true, too, there must have been a reason. Oh, God, what am I supposed to do?

He glanced at his watch. "Come on, Chris, let's not do this out here in the street. We'll go to the hotel, get a pizza."

I was trying to get one thing to make sense in the cha-os that was my brain. I felt like I was in a shipwreck in a storm at sea—everything I grabbed at was slippery and I just kept going under. My old self would just do what my father said, because I knew what would happen if I didn't. And then I thought, *Wait. I don't know what will happen, because I always do what my father says.* I didn't know what the consequences of disobedience were in any way. But I was still trying to sort out who to trust. Everything my father said sounded reasonable. He wasn't acting angry at all. And I didn't know thing one about my mother.

Trust. Who to trust. Sometimes when I trusted people, it turned out well, sometimes badly. Though I should have known better than to trust Cam when I knew he was lying to me, and I should have known better with Moth, too, when I knew she was an orange thief. I know better than to steal rides, and I know better than to steal food from farmers. My dad is in the category with Cam and Moth. He stole me.

"Here," I said. "Now."

"You don't know what you're letting yourself in for." My father glanced along the street. "Your mother is a very stubborn woman, very controlling, very rigid. Look how she still lives in the same apartment. Is that any way to move on?"

She stayed in the apartment because she was waiting for me. (At least I knew I had the right address!) *She waited for me on TV. She looked for me.* I wondered again why my father had really taken me, since he never seemed to want me for much of anything, just victory over her, maybe. *Stubborn, controlling … rigid?*

"You sound like you're describing yourself."

"Come on, Chris, Ramsay men stick together. I've told you enough; now let's go and I'll fill you in on the rest. You hungry? You must be hungry." He glanced along the street again.

Why was he glancing along the street? Then it clicked— he was afraid of getting caught. My father was a wanted kidnapper. "No. Here. Now. I told you."

"Chris, don't you speak to me in that tone of voice." He

was stern, his jaw was rigid, and he checked his watch again. "Now, get in the car and let's go!"

"I don't believe you have anything else to say. It's not 'complicated'—you just want to win. If I've learned anything in the past few days, it's to trust my instincts, and my instinct says 'stay.' She must be coming home from work soon, the way you keep looking at your watch, so I'm going to stay here and see for myself."

My father looked incredibly angry. Now his whole body was rigid and he was turning a bit red, but he said nothing. I still didn't know if I was making the right choice, and then I thought of what to do. "Stay with me. We'll all three sort it out."

"Get in that car immediately, if you know what's good for you. You're still a boy, and I'm still your father, so do as I say!"

"Oh, I know what's good for me. What's good for me is finding out the truth. What's good for me is not being lied to my whole life. You stole me! You stole my mother, you even stole you, because I respected you once and now I don't even know who you are!" I was shaking, but not from fear. It was the strangest feeling of ... power?

He went for the resigned shake of the head thing again, though he really couldn't pull it off. "After all I've done for you! Protected you from that witch!" His anger was rising again. "Raised you on my own! Bought you what you needed, cooked your food, bandaged your skinned knees." I felt a twinge for just a second but decided I wasn't buying. I just stared at him.

"Fine, you stubborn little brat! You're just like your mother!" He glanced down the street again. He was yelling a little now, his eyes wide. "Stay here, then, find out what she's like. You'll be crawling home before long. You'll take your chances whether I'm still there! Last offer!" He stood for a moment by the open door.

I kept my voice quiet and spoke slowly. "And what's so bad about cooking Minute Rice if I'm late? That's why we have it in the house."

My father slammed the passenger door. He crossed to the driver's side and slumped into the driver's seat and drove off in a tantrum of squealing rubber.

As I watched him disappear around the corner, I felt a surge of victory. But it didn't last long. I turned and looked at number 388 again. This wasn't quite finished yet. I felt good about standing up to my father. But what if I'd got it wrong? What *was* my mother like?

I went up to the building and tried the main door. It was open but the inner door was locked. I checked the directory. There it was. *Y. Coleman, Apartment 2D.*

Maybe she was actually in there now. It seemed like my dad thought she'd be coming from work, but I didn't know if he *knew* that. I stood for a moment. I realized I was shaking a little. Did I dare? By raising my finger and pressing a button, I was about to change everything in my life—and in someone else's life, too. Oh, who was I kidding? Everything in my life was already changed.

I thought about it. With the press of a button, I would no longer be lost on the road, I would be at home ... where I belonged, with my mother. My mother that I barely knew and had never really lived with. Even the two words together in my mind felt funny. *My. Mother.* Oh, why hadn't I just gone to the police in the first place, like Brian said? Curse my stupid father for passing on to me his distrust of cops—I knew where it came from now, anyway. He'd said I'd take my chances if I came back to Dallas. So what would happen next? Would he run away? Hm. Probably.

Just like I did.

No. I ran *to.*

I pressed the buzzer.

There was no reply.

After a few minutes, I rang again, harder.

Still no reply.

I checked my watch. Four o'clock. She probably *was* still at work, coming home soon, like my father had supposed. I figured I would have to wait. I started to slide down the wall to sit on my pack, and then decided it wasn't such a good idea to wait in the vestibule. If another tenant came out, or the superintendent, they'd probably question me, or throw me out, or call the police.

Just then, I saw someone coming down the hall. Maybe this could work.

It was a woman and, as she came nearer, I folded my hand-drawn map closed, hoping it looked like an envelope I might be delivering. She came through the door and I kind of touched my cap—to look polite and respectable, but more to obscure my face.

It worked. I was inside. I could smell cabbage, spices, and laundry. The carpet was worn but clean. It was easy to find Apartment 2D. It was up half a flight of stairs, at the back right of the floor. I tried knocking just in case the buzzer had been out, but there was still no answer. But I'd hoped for alcoves at the doorways and there were none. There was no way I could stand in the hall of this apartment building for an hour or more and not attract attention. I didn't think I needed to be inside, anyway, just somewhere

I could keep watch without being arrested for loitering. To be arrested now, so close. Probably my dad was reporting me as a runaway and they'd be here any minute. Oh, no, wait, he couldn't do that and not get arrested himself. Still, I was jumpy. There must be somewhere outside the building that I could go out of sight or, failing that, a park nearby where I could wait. I went back outside to scout.

I moved along the right side of the building. On each of the three floors above ground level, there were two balconies, one for the B apartments and one for the D apartments. If I could just get up on the balcony without being seen, I'd be pretty much safe. There was enough clutter on Y. Coleman's balcony that once I was up there, if I stayed pretty still, I'd probably not be noticed. I checked around all the windows in the neighborhood that I could see and didn't notice anyone looking out. No need to get arrested for attempted burglary—because that's what it would look like. I slipped off my backpack to test how to get onto this balcony. I jumped up and found I could grab the railing. Now, if I could do that with my backpack on, I'd be all set. I shouldered it back on.

I missed on the first try, but made it on the second. Fortunately, the wall of the building was flush with the balcony, so I could scramble higher, and then I was over the railing and tucked between a deck chair and a bicycle.

While I waited, I thought about my father's unexpected appearance. I realized that, as I had thought before, he would be paranoid about me finding out what had really happened. I didn't believe him that he was going to tell me when I turned sixteen—I was pretty sure he was just saying that to get me in the car. It wasn't our car, so I figured he must have flown to Toronto or maybe Buffalo and rented it. I suppose he just expected me to do as I was told and he'd take me home. I wondered whether I'd ever see him again.

It was boring, sitting so still on the balcony, and I was exhausted, and, in spite of my tension, or maybe just to escape it, I dozed off. I woke with a start when a sudden brightness disturbed me. A light was on in Apartment 2D. I leaned forward slowly, still mostly hidden by the deck chair, and peeked inside.

Walking across the room, carrying groceries in plastic bags and also a cloth bag, was a woman, about the right age to be my mother, with curlyish sandy hair like mine. My heart was pounding. Even if I hadn't known that it was her, I recognized her! I remembered her. I felt a tidal wave of emotion rush through me.

What should I do now? Probably go back down and ring the bell like a proper person. But if she came on the intercom, what would I say? "Hi, it's your son?" Too weird.

Just then, she turned, and I knew she'd seen me. I crawled out from my hiding spot, kneeling in front of the sliding glass doors with my hands out, to show her she could trust me.

I suddenly saw myself as she must have. I was filthy, bloodstained, grubby-looking. She stumbled backwards towardstoward the door. I shook my head wildly. She was reaching for the phone on a small table at the entrance. She must think I'm some crazed rapist, I realized.

"No, no!" I wasn't sure if she could hear me through the glass. I reached for my pack. She fumbled the phone and scrambled to pick it up. I knew she probably thought I was going for a weapon or something. From the pocket in the front of the pack, I pulled out the picture, Santa with the kid in the gooberish-looking snowsuit, slapped it against the window, pointed to myself.

My mother clasped the receiver of the phone to her chest. Was she having a heart attack? That would be just the thing after all this, to kill my own mother. But then she came to the glass and looked at me, and, just faintly, I could hear her, amazed, saying, "Benji?"

The next bit was a real blur. Of course, it took me only something like an hour to remember that my middle name was Benjamin, except it turns out Chris, or rather Christopher, is really my middle name. Seems my dad had switched them around—to throw them off the scent, I suppose.

My mom was crying and everything, and sort of touching me like I wasn't real, and she couldn't say anything coherent, just kept looking at me. Finally, she calmed down enough to say a real sentence. "I guess we should call the police."

My heart nearly stopped. After all that? She was going to send me back?

I stood frozen as she crossed to the phone.

"They'll need to be informed that you're *home*."

I started to breathe again.

She made the call but never took her eyes off me. Then she noticed my hand.

"Oh, you're hurt. Go wash your hand and I'll find a bandage."

I looked around, having no idea where a bathroom might be.

"Oh, down the hall on the right."

I went into the bathroom and closed the door. My face in the medicine cabinet mirror looked back at me. The usual inventory: freckles, blue eyes, sandy hair. I must have inherited them from my mother. But it seemed I'd been computer-aged in real life. Inside and out.

Two police came—one was a policewoman. (I wondered if they were actually Mounties, but I didn't ask. They weren't wearing red coats, though, so probably not.) The policewoman asked ten million questions, but I just said I took a bus. I kind of thought they didn't really believe I got across the border that easy, but I just said, "Well, I did." I was a bit cleaned up since my arrival, so I guess it was kind of believable. I never told them about my dad following me and they never thought to ask that one.

After the police left, my mom made us some dinner— just spaghetti with sauce from a jar, but then she took out a block of hard cheese from the fridge and grated it, instead of shaking it from a can! It tasted pretty good. Of course, I was completely starving by that time.

We were kind of shy with each other at first and didn't talk much. I guess it was all too new for both of us. I started to dry the dishes after she washed them, but she said, "No, no, just leave them. They'll dry."

"Um .. m ..." I was having trouble calling her Mom or

Mother or whatever. "I know it's long distance, but I'd kind of like to phone my friend Brian back in Dallas to tell him I made it."

"Sure, sweetheart. Don't worry about the cost. Talk as long as you need to." She even left the room so I could talk privately.

Brian himself picked up the phone.

"Hello?"

"Hi, Brian, it's me, Chris."

"Chris! How are you? *Where* are you?"

"Um ... I'm in my mother's apartment in Kingston."

"Wow, what took you so long? I thought you'd be like two days! It's Wednesday already!"

"Well, some of the plans didn't go so smoothly ..." I didn't really want to get into all of it. "So how're y'all doin' down there?" (Whoa, Texas much?) "Did anyone notice I was gone?"

"I think your father must have called you in sick to school, because nobody seemed too worried. Man, everyone is going to freak *out* when I tell them what really happened!"

Suddenly, I didn't want to be on the phone with Brian. I could picture the way everyone would be amazed by the story of me seeing myself on TV and taking off, but having just lived what happened *next* was exhausting. I knew they would think it was cool, but I knew if I ever heard such a story, I would understand it in a way they couldn't. And I still had a lot to figure out.

"Brian? It's long distance, so I can't really talk long. I just wanted to let you know I'm okay and to say thanks for your help. I'll get you your money back when I can."

"Take your time."

"Thanks. Say hi to everyone from me. In Canadianese."

Brian laughed.

"I'll write you a letter soon, once I know what's going on."

"Okay. Take care, buddy!"

"You, too."

E ven after two weeks, I'm only starting to get my mind around everything. One of the first things I did was send a quick "I'm okay, plus thank you for saving my life" card to Beatrice. Hallmark doesn't seem to make one, so I had to write it myself.

It's harder to write to Brian. I thought I was going to explain everything to him, but I can't. I *said* I'd write him, though, so here goes:

Dear Brian,

How are things?

Things here are gradually becoming normal. It turns out that my mom has an extra bedroom in her place, so once we got a bed, I fitted right in there, physically. And personally, too, though that took a little longer. At first, my mom couldn't get over me. She just kept looking at me like I was from another planet, and I guess I was. She's still totally freaked by my Texas accent. People here talk all fast and short, almost Englishy. It's cute, though.

Living with my mom is really different from living with

my father—I can see why they split up. She's fun and doesn't get on my case about stuff, though I guess when she gets used to me, I'll stop being the King of Siam around here. It's pretty cool, though. We laugh at the same jokes. We laugh! She gives me an allowance and I set up a bank account, so I should be able to save some up to pay you back.

My mom works as a secretary at the university here— that's what they call it, not college (see what I mean about them being Englishy?)—and she arranged to get a bunch of time off in the summer so we can get to know each other, she says. She wants to go camping. Pretty cool, huh?

She's teaching me some fancy cooking, but tonight I'm making your mom's Texas five-alarm chili for us. She said she's alarmed and she'll make a salad.

School here is okay. It's too late for me to go out for baseball, but I went to a couple of the games, and I'm pretty sure I'll make the team next year. Compared to our team, these guys basically suck. There are some cute girls here, but I haven't met them yet. Oh, and guess what—I've grown an inch—I mean, two-point-five centimeters!

I hope you had fun at Paula's party. Tell her hi. Maybe you could come up and visit sometime. It's different here. I can't explain exactly how. Like different candy bars and stuff.

I heard my dad left our house. I guess he's hiding somewhere else now. I mean, I have a lot of thinking to do about everything that happened. I don't think I hate him or want him to rot in jail or anything. But I don't miss him. Not at all.

Well, gotta go. Write back. Say hi to everyone.
Yours truly,
Chris (yes, my mom is getting used to it)

My mom taps on my door just as I finish signing my name.

"Knock, knock," she's giggling.

I roll my eyes but play along. "Who's there?"

"Ayla."

"Ayla who?"

"Ayla View."

"Ha-ha! I love you, too, Mom."

"C'mon, Chris. Let's go make dinner."

ACKNOWLEDGMENTS

Many thanks to all my teachers: I would like especially to thank Derek McDermott for showing me my feet and all my students at Alexander Mackenzie High School (plus Claire) for showing me what to do with them. Special thanks to Peter Carver for his belief in this project and all his help.

Photo courtesy of James Pacitto

The issue of missing children is an unfortunate reality today in our world. I'm interested in what it was that inspired you to tell Chris's story. Was it the issue itself, or the idea of a character who had been put in this situation?

I actually started with the idea of an adventure story, like *Treasure Island*. After visiting Robert Louis Stevenson's honeymoon spot in California, I was wondering about how a young person in modern times could be forced out on his (or her) own and left to fend for himself, like Jim Hawkins. Later the same day, I spotted *The Face on the Milk Carton* by Carolyn Cooney in a bookstore and thought, "That could be a reason a kid would take off." What kid hasn't imagined at some moment that their parents aren't really their parents and that they are really a prince or princess who was abducted? The issue of parental custody battles was in the news at the time (not that it was any more something that happened than at any other time, just that it had become a hot issue), and the whole concept clicked together in that moment. I began writing that very day. But it was twenty years before this book finally came together as a fully realized story.

As you worked on the story over the years, how did it change and develop? How did the character of Chris grow on you? What did you learn about his story as you continued to write it?

The biggest change over the time I spent with the story was switching it from third person—as it was written in the first draft—to first person, as suggested by a participant in a workshop course I took on writing for children. When I made that switch, Chris became more alive. A number of young people (boys and girls) I've met as a teacher or in other circumstances have been an inspiration for the character. Of course, it's all very well to write an adventure story, but modern readers also need to know what's going on in the heads of their main characters, and that was an area I have worked on bringing out. Although I always felt I knew Chris, I discovered that I needed to show more for readers to know him, too.

You were involved in the TV series, *The Kids of Degrassi Street* and *Degrassi Junior High/Degrassi High*, writing scripts for the series, and also two of the novels arising out of the series. How did that experience affect your telling this story?

I learned to write on Degrassi. For one, I was the publicist for the series, so I had to write story synopses for the press releases. Taking a story down to its ultimate bare bones—what we called the "*TV Guide*" version of the story—was enlightening. Secondly, writing scripts and novels for the original *Degrassi Junior High* and *Degrassi High* put me through the hoops and taught me structure. Structure is essential to a good story, I think. And third, the many, many drafts of a script or manuscript taught me two things: 1. You *have* to make it as good as it can be. 2. You can. First draft is only the beginning.

Chris is a fifteen-year-old who has never been called upon to make a major decision in his young life, due to the control exerted by his father. But, in your story, he has to make many crucial decisions that are going to affect his life. As a teacher of high school students, how competent do you think teenagers today are in taking important initiatives in their lives?

When I was reading this to my Writer's Craft class, one of my students commented, "This is a very resourceful kid." I think all kids are resourceful. You might think that Chris has never been put to the test before, so how can he do this? But I think that, put to the test, all people try to do what they need to do. People, including kids, are survival machines. Think of the Five Children who met It, Sara Crewe, Holden Caulfield, Huckleberry Finn, and also all the true stories of people who have strived. Anne Frank is one we remember, but every person who has faced adversity, whether they won or lost in the end, has fought with everything they could.

What do you think motivated Chris's father to "steal" his child from his mother? As you were writing this story, did you research similar kidnappings by parents who decided to abduct their own children for similar reasons?

There are several things we don't know, because Chris doesn't know. He speculates on some of it, but if anything's not in the book, I am not going to cheat and tell you things he can't know. You decide. I hope I've left enough clues for you.

You started writing this story in the early 1990s, which accounts for its being set in that period. How different would the story be if it were set in contemporary times?

I would be writing a different book if I started it now. It's amazing how much has changed in our world in that period of time. Few people in 1992 had a cell phone; the World Trade Center was still standing; we'd barely heard of the "information super-highway." Chris's relatively easy crossing of the border into Canada was still believable back then. But I was actually able to do research using the Internet that wouldn't have been possible in the early 1990s. This book owes a debt to Google, Wikipedia, and many other Web sites and services online. My grandmother was born before the Wright Brothers flew and was alive not only to know that people landed on the moon, but to see it live on television. The world is a lively place, so it's fun to

hold down a year or a week and see wha
and the Toronto Blue Jays did win the World. Oh,

n 1992.

How has your being a writer affected the w
you approach teaching young people? hich

It's made me get behind in marking as I focus
ing! You should see the pile of marking I have! But re it-
don't see them as separate activities. I love people and I
to try to figure out what goes on in their minds, what mo
vates them. Making fictitious characters is a cross betwee
taking what I know of young people already and making
up the kind of people I would like to know and deciding
what goes on behind their eyes. It's like playing with dolls,
only way better, because it's amazing how often they'll do
things that surprise you, and characters show up that you
weren't expecting, and you have to improvise what your
main character will do in response, just as everyone constantly does in real, everyday life.

What advice would you give young writers, in light of
the evolving media world of today?

The inhabitants of the universe will never tire of stories.
You might be reading this in a book from the store or a
book from the library, or on an electronic reader, or hearing it read to you by a person live or on some recorded version, or on a medium we haven't thought of yet. Maybe
you are a resident of another planet who has found this in

l outer space. I doubt you are read-

what we ear ou didn't enjoy Chris's story, so, thank

ing this int ve a good story, well told. You can learn

you, "read y paying attention to your world, reading,

how to d ring, and paying attention to how people

practic what you write. If you are a writer of any age,

respo m doesn't matter. Think of a good story and tell

the

it w

hold down a year or a week and see what it was doing. Oh, and the Toronto Blue Jays did win the World Series in 1992.

How has your being a writer affected the ways in which you approach teaching young people?

It's made me get behind in marking as I focus on writing! You should see the pile of marking I have! But really, I don't see them as separate activities. I love people and love to try to figure out what goes on in their minds, what motivates them. Making fictitious characters is a cross between taking what I know of young people already and making up the kind of people I would like to know and deciding what goes on behind their eyes. It's like playing with dolls, only way better, because it's amazing how often they'll do things that surprise you, and characters show up that you weren't expecting, and you have to improvise what your main character will do in response, just as everyone constantly does in real, everyday life.

What advice would you give young writers, in light of the evolving media world of today?

The inhabitants of the universe will never tire of stories. You might be reading this in a book from the store or a book from the library, or on an electronic reader, or hearing it read to you by a person live or on some recorded version, or on a medium we haven't thought of yet. Maybe you are a resident of another planet who has found this in what we earthlings call outer space. I doubt you are reading this interview if you didn't enjoy Chris's story, so, thank you, "readers." I love a good story, well told. You can learn how to do that by paying attention to your world, reading, practicing, sharing, and paying attention to how people respond to what you write. If you are a writer of any age, the medium doesn't matter. Think of a good story and tell it well.